SPECIAL MESSAGE TO READERS

This book is published by
THE ULVERSCROFT FOUNDATION
a registered charity in the U.K., No. 264873

The Foundation was established in 1974 to provide funds to help towards research, diagnosis and treatment of eye diseases. Below are a few examples of contributions made by THE ULVERSCROFT FOUNDATION:

A new Children's Assessment Unit at Moorfield's Hospital, London.

•

Twin operating theatres at the Western Ophthalmic Hospital, London.

•

The Frederick Thorpe Ulverscroft Chair of Ophthalmology at the University of Leicester.

•

Eye Laser equipment to various eye hospitals.

If you would like to help further the work of the Foundation by making a donation or leaving a legacy, every contribution, no matter how small, is received with gratitude. Please write for details to:

**THE ULVERSCROFT FOUNDATION,
The Green, Bradgate Road, Anstey,
Leicester LE7 7FU. England
Telephone: (0533) 364325**

THE NURSE WAS JULIET

When the stranger whirled into her little mountain town changes began. Change in the way she and her doctor mother conducted their small clinic. Change in her fiancé, till now the most dependable thing in Nurse Juliet's life. Most frightening of all — change in her heart. How could she hate everything about the man — and still dream about him all the time?

*Books by Peggy Gaddis
in the Linford Romance Library:*

NURSE'S CHOICE
EVERGLADES NURSE
CAROLINA LOVE SONG
NURSE AT THE CEDARS
A NURSE CALLED HAPPY
NURSE ANGELA
NURSE AT SPANISH CAY

PEGGY GADDIS

THE NURSE WAS JULIET

Complete and Unabridged

LINFORD
Leicester

First published in the
United States of America in 1966 by
Macfadden-Bartell Corporation, New York

First Linford Edition
published February 1991

Copyright © 1965 by Arcadia House
All rights reserved

British Library CIP Data

Gaddis, Peggy
 The nurse was Juliet.—Large print ed.—
 Linford romance library
 I. Title
 813.52 [F]

ISBN 0–7089–6977–1

Published by
F. A. Thorpe (Publishing) Ltd.
Anstey, Leicestershire

Set by Words & Graphics Ltd.
Anstey, Leicestershire
Printed and bound in Great Britain by
T. J. Press (Padstow) Ltd., Padstow, Cornwall

1

JULIET COCHRAN, R.N. brought the jeep to a halt and sat for a moment with her hands wearily poised on the wheel. Ahead of her, the makeshift road, which was little more than a twisting, winding steeply rising mule track, had ended abruptly. At the very top of the hill, an ancient cabin was tucked beneath an overhanging cliff as though it had crept there for protection against the bitter winds of winter and the storms of summer. And in that small cabin was Miss Sarah Smithwick, Juliet's last call of the morning.

She regarded the path that she had to climb and drew a resigned breath, thankful that Miss Sarah required only a weekly visit from the public health nurse attached to the clinic at Haleyville, eleven tortuous miles back down that makeshift road.

She got out of the jeep, drew her heavy cape about her and shivered. For though the calendar said it was May, and down in the valley at the foot of the mountain spring was already visible, it was still winter up here. Even though mountain laurel fringed the banks of the small, brawling creek, and clumps of wild azaleas made splashes of color against the dark hills, up here at the mountain's timberline the wind was still cold, with an edge of ice in its teeth, and she was glad to see that a plume of smoke floated above the chimney of the small, sturdy-looking old cabin.

She slipped the worn strap of her medical case over her shoulder and turned back to pick up the large package of mail, mostly circulars. The most imposing part was a batch of Sunday newspapers, and she grinned ruefully as she hefted the weight of the bundle and started up the steep path.

By the time she reached the top, the door of the cabin had opened and a woman stood waiting for her. She was tall, spare, her graying hair twisted into a tight knot at the back of her head, and she was dressed in an immaculately clean percale dress with hand-crocheted 'lace' at wrists and neck. The woman's eyes were shining eagerly behind her old-fashioned steel-rimmed spectacles, and she greeted Juliet with a warmth that came straight from an eager, grateful heart.

"I do declare, Julie, you're a sight for sore eyes, and I'm that glad to see you! Come in, come in. You must be just about frozen. It's still a mite chilly outside," the woman chattered happily as she drew Juliet into the cabin.

"A mite chilly is the understatement of the century, Miss Sarah." Juliet laughed. "And it's not I that am a sight for sore eyes. It's the Sunday papers you know I'm bringing you."

Miss Sarah laughed, accepted the papers Juliet handed her and cradled them in her arms as though the bundle had been something alive and tenderly loved. She looked up at Juliet with an abashed light in her eyes.

"I reckon you think I'm a mite silly, Julie, to want to read the Sunday papers, especially the one from New York," she offered a tacit apology. "But I do get a sight of pleasure out of them. I truly do."

"Then there's surely no reason in the world you shouldn't have them, Miss Sarah, and every reason you should," Juliet assured her firmly.

Miss Sarah was still cradling the bundle of papers in her arms, and she said shyly, "Well, when I sold those handmade quilts down at Haleyville last summer, I decided I'd put part of the money into a subscription for this New York paper. And I've never been sorry, either!"

"Well, why should you be? The quilts were yours. You'd made them yourself out of scraps you'd saved for years, and if that woman felt they were worth twenty-five dollars apiece, then you surely had the right to use the money for anything you wanted. And if part of it went for something that gives you as much pleasure as your Sunday paper, then hooray for you!"

"You don't think I'm a fool, Julie?" asked Miss Sarah anxiously.

Juliet's eyebrows went up, and she stared at the woman in honest amazement.

"You, Miss Sarah? I think you're the bravest, smartest, gentlest and finest woman I know, and I only wish I had half your courage," Juliet answered.

Miss Sarah seemed surprised.

"Courage, Julie? You mean living here all-soul-alone like I do? Land alive, Julie, that don't take courage. What would take courage would be for me to live somewhere with people all around me. That would purely scare me to death," she protested. "I do like my privacy, Julie."

Juliet looked out of the small window, neatly curtained in spotless, neatly starched red and white checked gingham, and saw the mountains rearing themselves against a distant sky. In all that expanse of trees and mountains and space, there was not the faintest sign of a human habitation. The makeshift road had ended there; beyond that place there was only wilderness and mountains.

"Well, Miss Sarah, privacy you have really got, not to say isolation," she admitted, opened her bag and took out her blood-pressure kit. "Roll up your sleeve. Not that I think there is anything at all the matter with your blood pressure, but since I'm here we might as well check."

Miss Sarah laid the papers down, still touching them as though they were alive and dearly beloved, and bared her scrawny arm. When Julie had completed her examination, she dropped her instruments back in the bag and said, smiling warmly, "You have the blood pressure of a girl, Miss Sarah, and your heart is sound as a dollar used to be! In short, you're in perfect condition."

Miss Sarah beamed happily as she drew down her sleeve and buttoned the cuff with its neat adornment of hand-crocheted 'lace'.

"I'm that glad, Julie," she said happily. "It will soon be time for me to get my garden in if I plan to eat next winter."

"And of course you do." Juliet smiled at her. "But take it easy this year, Miss Sarah. Don't overplant and wear yourself out. Promise?"

Miss Sarah's eyes twinkled.

"You mean like I did last year, Julie?" She grinned like an impish child. "Well, not a scrap of what I raised last year was wasted. Nettie Hicks came up and helped me, and we canned up a storm! And the Hicks folks was mighty glad to share what I had. They don't have much to eat, what with Ben Hicks being such a worthless no-good sort of fellow and that raft of young ones they have."

She hesitated a moment, and then she added, "Nettie would be tickled pink to come and live with me permanent, and Ben would be mighty glad to get rid of her. Sometimes I feel right mean that I don't ask Nettie to come. Julie, I guess I'm just a cross-grained old woman, but I've lived here alone so long I just don't know how I'd make out with somebody else in the house. Nettie's salt of the earth and as good as they come. But she *does* like to talk."

Juliet laughed and squeezed Miss Sarah's scrawny shoulder affectionately.

"How right you are, Miss Sarah," she agreed. "And unless you really want her here, don't you dare ask her. Of course, it's nice to know that if you really needed her, she would be available."

Miss Sarah nodded soberly.

"I know," she admitted. "That's what makes me feel so mean. I know I could get her if I was to take sick or get hurt. But I don't want her when I am able to do for myself."

"You're not mean, Miss Sarah. Stop downgrading yourself. This is your home, and you have a perfect right to have it any way you want it. But I am glad and relieved to know that Nettie is available if you do need her. And I know how gladly she would serve you. And now

I have to run. Afternoon clinic hours will be starting by the time I get back to town."

"Wait a minute; I haven't paid you," protested Miss Sarah. She brought out a small change purse from her apron pocket and carefully fished out a quarter which she held out proudly to Juliet, who accepted it as if she were being well paid for her service.

Miss Sarah walked with her to the door and said hospitably, "It's always a real pleasure to see you, Julie. How's Dr. Laura?"

"Oh, Mother's fine," Juliet answered. "I'll see you next Monday, Miss Sarah. And of course you know that if you need me before then, you have only to let me know."

"I do, Julie, I do. And I'm mighty grateful for the knowledge," Miss Sarah told her happily, and watched as Juliet went down the trail to the waiting jeep.

When Juliet reached the foot of the path, she turned and saw Miss Sarah was still in the open doorway. Juliet threw up her hand in a gesture of leavetaking and saw Miss Sarah go back into the house and close the door.

Negotiating with extreme caution the turning of the jeep for the homeward journey, Juliet's mind clung for a little while to the old woman. Miss Sarah had lived in that cabin since girlhood. There had been a year or two when she had gone away; no one knew where. She had been a radiantly lovely young girl, legend had it, and her parents had lived in the cabin. When she came back two years later, her mother was dead, and Sarah and her father had continued to live here. Her father was paralyzed by a lumbering accident, and Miss Sarah nursed him with great devotion. Even then they had discouraged visitors. By the time the old man died, people had all but forgotten that Miss Sarah had ever been away at all. She had gone on living alone in the old cabin, with chickens, a pig or two each spring, and a garden that she had tended alone and with such industry that each summer she had been able to can and preserve enough food to last her through the winter. No one knew how she managed to have any cash. But she seemed always to have what was absolutely necessary. She brought her eggs to Haleyville and had traded them for coffee, sugar and tea; apparently she needed nothing else that she did not raise for herself.

She was civil, courteous, but very aloof, discouraging any attempts at friendliness. The only odd fact was one that people had long ago forgotten was odd: the fact that she subscribed to a New York Sunday newspaper. As long as she was able to get to Haleyville, she herself had collected her mail, which chiefly consisted of the Sunday paper. But after Juliet had come back from Atlanta, a graduate R.N., and had taken on the public health visiting nurse assignment for the county, Juliet had collected her mail and brought it to her along with whatever food or other supplies she had needed. And Miss Sarah had thankfully retired from any contact with the outside world.

People in and around Haleyville had long ago ceased to wonder about Miss Sarah and her affairs, which was, obviously, exactly the way Miss Sarah wanted it! Only Nettie Hicks, a widowed mountain woman who, because she had no other place to live, shared a very crowded cabin with her married son and his large family, was friendly with Miss Sarah.

As she drove down the narrow, twisting road to town, Juliet wondered why the two could not live together. It would have been a wonderful solution to poor Nettie's situation as an unwelcome but overworked member of her son's family. However, Juliet agreed with Miss Sarah that Nettie was a talker, and Miss Sarah cherished her privacy so much —

Juliet broke off her reverie as she saw a man sitting beside the road ahead, his attitude one of utter exhaustion. He wore the usual mountain garb. The cool wind blew his ragged white whiskers, and his stout stick lay beside him.

She drew the jeep to a halt beside him and leaned out.

"Were you waiting for me, Gran'pa Elson?" she called.

The old man's face lit up, and he struggled to his feet.

"Well, now, Miss Julie, I reckon I shore was," he agreed. "I'm a mite ashamed, though. Know I ought to be able to hoof the whole way, but seems like my old legs ain't as good as they used to be."

"They will wear out on a fellow, won't they?" Juliet laughed as she waited for him to clamber into the jeep. "I'm so glad I happened along and saved you the rest of the hike. You're almost halfway there, though, and I'm sure you would have made it."

"Well, now, thankee for saying that, Miss Julie. I'm right obliged for your kindness," the old man answered, and heaved a contented sigh as he straightened his legs as much as the confines of the jeep would permit. "You been seeing

Miss Sarah, I reckon? Hope she's up and doing well?"

"Oh, yes, she's fine, as usual," Juliet answered.

The old man stared straight ahead as the jeep negotiated the steep road, with the sheer mountain on one side, the steep drop to the valley on the other.

"I'm right glad to hear that," he said politely. "I allus wondered where in tarnation she went that time she just sort of vanished from these parts. Nobody knew a thing about it. Her Maw and Paw never said a blessed word about it. One day she was here; next day she wasn't. Folks was all mighty curious, I can tell you. She was a mighty pretty girl, too. Folks told a lot of tales about her running off with some 'flat-land furriner,' but nobody never could prove nothing or make any of the tales stick."

"Well, where she went and why she went really concerns nobody but Miss Sarah, now does it, Gran'pa?" Juliet tried to speak lightly but could not quite keep the edge out of her voice.

"It all happened many years ago, before I was born. I've known her ever since I came back from my training course, and I'm convinced that whatever happened does her no discredit. Miss Sarah is good and decent and honest, and all she asks is that people leave her alone."

The old man shot her a faintly quizzical glance, attesting that he had caught the reproof in her voice.

"Well, folks sure do that," he drawled. "Reckon wouldn't nobody climb up there to that place where she lives 'less they was mighty fond of her or she needed them mighty bad. O' course if she did, reckon all the folks hereabouts would be going up there to do what they could for her."

"I'm sure they would, Gran'pa," Juliet answered. The edge was gone from her voice, and she felt a little ashamed that she had struck out at him in defense of Miss Sarah.

"Folks in these parts allus thought a heap of Mr. Smithwick," the old man mused aloud. "A great fellow to keep to hisself; reckon maybe that's where Miss Sarah got wanting to be left alone from."

"I should imagine," Juliet agreed, and waved at a man and woman who were plodding down the road ahead of her. She leaned out and called, "Want a lift?"

The two looked eagerly at her, saw the old man sitting smugly beside her and stepped back, an expression of chilliness touching their faces.

"We're obliged, Miss Julie, but we can make it all right," the man answered stiffly. "Ain't more'n a mile further."

Juliet waved an acknowledgment, knowing that it was hostility to the old man beside her that had caused them to refuse the lift. And she knew, too, that the old man recognized it, for she heard him chuckle dryly as she drove on.

"That Lafe Jenkins and his old woman is a couple o' fools," said Gran'pa dryly. "He works over at the sawmill and just comes home Saturday and Sunday. And that's a good-looking woman he's got."

Juliet said stiffly, "Gran'pa, you're a

wicked old gossip, and we both know it. And if I hear one more word around town about Miss Sarah, I'm going to know who started it. And if I do, the next 'shot' I give you will be with a blunt needle!"

The old man turned shocked, startled eyes on her.

"You wouldn't do that, Miss Julie. Them 'shots' hurt bad enough when the needle's sharp. Dunno as I could take 'em with a blunt needle," he protested.

"Well, you'll find out if I hear you spreading any loose talk around town about Miss Sarah, or Maude Jenkins, or anybody else," Juliet threatened him ominously. "You remember that now."

"Yessum, I reckon I will," the old man answered with a trace of humility. "Be all right if I talk to folks about this here murder trial that's gonna start here next week?"

With a glint in her eye, Juliet told him firmly, "You certainly may, Gran'pa, and I'll help you!"

Gran'pa shot her a swift glance.

"Miss Julie, how come you reckon them folks over to the county seat sent that there trial over here? It wa'n't none o' our doing, Jim Blayne gettin' killed and all," he demanded.

"The defendant's lawyers claimed they couldn't get a fair trial for their man at the county seat because people were too worked up over the murder. So they asked for a change of venue, and the judge granted it," Juliet explained.

"Well, I reckon they was right," Gran'pa answered vigorously. "Fellow don't deserve no trial. Folks ought to take him out and hang him. He's as guilty as sin, and ever'body knows it."

"But he's entitled to a fair trial, Gran'pa, under the law."

"Funny kind of law that lets a fellow murder somebody that's been good to him same as Jim Blayne was to this varmint," Gran'pa said. "Wasn't a finer man nowheres than Jim Blayne. He give a job to this wuthless no-good, and when he caught the fellow robbin' him, all he was gonna do was have him arrested.

And the fellow slugged him and then put him in Jim's own truck and drove out in the woods and set fire to the truck. And the law's wastin' the county's time and money and folk's patience trying the man!"

His tone of utter disgust expressed what Juliet knew was the feeling of the entire county. But she only said, "According to law, Gran'pa, he's innocent until proven guilty in a regular court."

"Well, they ought to try him where it happened; not drag their dirty doings over here to a law-abidin' place like Haleyville," Gran'pa insisted. "Why, we ain't had a murder trial in Haleyville in I dunno when. Only troubles we have are chicken stealin's and Saturday night ruckuses at the Crumps' place."

Juliet silently agreed with him. As they approached the outskirts of the town, Gran'pa went on thoughtfully, "Reckon they'll be a lot o' strangers in town for the trial; folks from the flat-lands that never heard tell o' Haleyville till they read about this in the newspapers. It'll be in the flat-land newspapers, won't it, Miss Julie?"

Juliet turned the nose of the jeep in through the entrance to the clinic and said dryly, "You can count on that, Gran'pa, In a great big way!"

She stopped the jeep beneath the giant oak that shaded the parking space, and Gran'pa climbed out stiffly. The big, rambling old white house faced the road and the steep rise of mountains across the creek. There were benches beneath some of the trees, and on these men sat waiting for the attention of Dr. Laura and of Juliet.

"I'm much obliged for the ride, Miss Julie," said Gran'pa, and went to join a group of three men on a bench near the house.

Juliet nodded and smiled at the men as she lifted out her bag and went into the house through the side entrance that led directly to Dr. Laura's office.

There was no one in the office, but in the examination room, which had once been the dining room of the big old house, she heard the murmur of voices and knew that Dr. Laura had already begun the afternoon clinic hours.

She put away her bag, hung up her cape and went on down the hall to the kitchen, where Mattie, vast and ebony-hued and immaculate in her dark print dress and white apron, greeted her affectionately.

"Reckon you ready for somethin' to eat, ain't you, honey?" said Mattie. "Well, you sit right down here and eat whilst everything is hot. You have a bad morning, honey?"

Juliet smiled gratefully at her and sniffed at the appetizing fragrance of the plate set before her.

"About the same as usual, Mattie. No better, no worse; just routine," she answered.

Mattie stood beside the table, her fists on her ample hips, and said quietly, "Folks is mighty riled up, Miss Julie, 'bout that man bein' brought here to be tried."

"I know, Mattie," Juliet answered.

"I picked up Gran'pa Elson on the road, and he was telling me how upset people were."

"Waitin' for you along the road like he always does, was he? The lazy, triflin' old so-and-so!"

"Now, Mattie," Juliet smiled in a faint reproof, "he's an old man, and feeble."

"Feeble?" Mattie scoffed. "He's an old man who trades on folks' pity, and the only thing about him that ain't feeble is that mean tongue o' his. Miss Julie, if you knew the kind of tales he spreads around — "

"I do, Mattie, and I warned him this morning that if I heard any more of them, I'd use a blunt needle when I gave him his next 'shot.' I think I scared him." Juliet grinned wickedly.

"Well, I hope you didn't just scare him; I hope you'll do it. Way past time for somebody to do something to shut his wicked old mouth."

"Well, let's hope I did, for a while, anyway," Juliet agreed. "Anyway, I don't think anybody will be talking about much of anything, or listening to much of anything, except this trial."

Mattie nodded and went back to the stove, where a pot of turnip greens was simmering. Before either of them could speak again, there was a brisk sound of footsteps in the hall, and the swinging door was pushed open to reveal Dr. Laura, tall, spare, harassed-looking. Then she saw Juliet, and her expression softened.

"Thank goodness you're back, darling," she said quickly. "Ev Perkins is here, and it seems Mamie's baby is due any minute and I have to hurry. Can you cope this afternoon while I'm away?"

Juliet was on her feet before Dr. Laura stopped speaking.

"But Mamie's baby isn't due for another week," she protested.

"Let's be grateful it decided to arrive in the daytime," Dr. Laura said ruefully. "That road to the Perkins place is not one I enjoy driving after dark. And Mamie always has her babies with a minimum of trouble. The midwife is with her. But

Mamie wants this baby delivered by an M.D., not by old Aunt Zilla."

"Mamie's got sense," Juliet agreed.

"Miss Laura, you ain't had a mouthful of vittles — " Mattie protested.

Dr. Laura smiled warmly at her.

"Oh, they may feed me at the Perkins place, and if they don't I'll be all right until I get back, Mattie," Dr. Laura answered, and sniffed. "Turnip greens? Mattie, you're a treasure. I don't know what we'd do without you."

"Well, long as I'm up and on my feet, you ain't gonna find out, neither," Mattie assured her firmly.

Juliet went with her mother back to the office, and there was a brief survey of the charts for the clinic patients due that afternoon. As Dr. Laura accepted the jeep keys and started for the door, she paused to say, "You're such a comfort to me, darling."

"Well, I should just hope so!" Juliet tried hard for a light note. "What else are daughters for?"

"Remind me to go into that with you

sometime when we have more time." Dr. Laura grinned at her and hurried out.

Juliet sat down at the desk for a moment and heard the jeep driving away. Then she sighed and looked down at the charts and stood up to summon the first patient, waiting anxiously in the big old reception room.

All afternoon, as she changed dressings, administered injections and attended to all the routine tasks that were a part of the clinic's afternoon schedule, her mind was busy with the thought of what the coming murder trial was going to mean to her beloved small home town.

Dr. Laura and Dr. Jeff Cochran had completed their internship at the same big hospital in Atlanta and had then come to the mountains, seeking a place where their services were needed. And to the vast delight and relief of Haleyville, they had settled in that small, isolated town tucked back into a fold of the Blue Ridge mountains. There they had practiced their profession happily and devotedly. There Juliet had been born and had grown up. Before her tenth birthday her father had died violently from the bite of a rabid fox; and Dr. Laura had squared her shoulders, set her teeth and gone on practicing the profession to which she and her adored husband had dedicated themselves, bringing up Juliet to revere the profession as much as they had.

Juliet had gone to Atlanta for her nurse's training, and every minute she'd been away from Haleyville, she had been homesick. After she won her R.N., she could not get back fast enough, and she had joined her mother in aiding the sick, the lame, the halt and the injured in the small town.

There was nothing about Haleyville that she wanted changed. The big city had sickened her, with its noise and clamor, and her service in the emergency ward of the big charity hospital had convinced her once and for all that she could never be happy or even satisfied anywhere but back in that small town tucked away in a fold of the mountains. People were friendly there, good neighbors who rallied instantly to the call of someone less fortunate than themselves; concerned for each other, perfectly content with their isolation and their quiet peace.

And now that quiet and peace were going to be invaded by an ugly murder trial, although Haleyville had no responsibility for the crime and should not have been called on to handle it. For years, Juliet knew, when people heard the name 'Haleyville,' they would say, "Oh, yes, that's where that terrible murder took place, wasn't it? That drifter was given a job and kindness by a man and showed his latitude by murdering the man and trying to burn his body to make it look like an accident."

There would be no way to convince such people that Haleyville had been merely the scene of the trial; not of the murder. And Juliet resented that fiercely, just as she resented the thought that curious, morbid-minded people would be drawn there by stories in the newspapers.

For she could not doubt that the Atlanta newspapers, and perhaps those from other large cities, would be sufficiently interested to send reporters to cover the trial.

She had to set her teeth hard and force the thoughts out of her mind while she attended the patients who had come for Dr. Laura's attention but accepted hers gratefully, with complete confidence in her ability to do what was required.

But not one of them, except the children, failed to mention the coming trial.

"I reckon your boy friend, Mr. Alden, will be one of the lawyers at the trial, won't he, Miss Julie?" one woman asked her.

"As a spectator only, I'm sure, Annie-Lou," Juliet answered.

"Well, of course I knowed he hadn't been hired by that no-good's lawyers. He's bringing big city lawyers up here to defend him, just as if we didn't have a mighty fine lawyer right here in town," Annie-Lou said as she winced at the needle going into her arm.

"I believe the state appointed his lawyer, Annie-Lou," Juliet told her. "It seems he had no money for a lawyer, and the law requires that a man be defended — "

"Well, it's too bad Jim Blayne didn't have somebody to defend him, seems to me like," Annie-Lou answered, and added, "Reckon I'd better be gettin' along. Sam and the young-'uns will be gettin' hungry. See you next week, Miss Julie."

"Be sure you do, Annie-Lou. We're getting that blood pressure down, and we want to keep it that way," Juliet warned her. "You watch your diet now, you hear me?"

Annie-Lou smiled warmly. "Oh, yessum, Miss Julie, I sure will."

It was dusk when Dr. Laura came back. She looked tired and at the same time pleased.

"Well, Ev has another plow-hand," she announced. "Mamie was afraid it was going to be a girl, and she says they have more than enough girls already. And I'm bound to agree with her. Seven girls and only one boy — until now. This makes two, and Ev is strutting like a rooster."

"Did you have anything to eat?" Juliet demanded sternly.

Dr. Laura looked startled.

"Now that you mention it, I don't believe I did," she admitted. "There didn't seem to be time."

"Well, you come straight to the kitchen and eat! Mattie cooked the greens with a ham hock and there's all sorts of other goodies. Since you insist on a proper diet for your patients, I can only say, 'Practice what you preach'," Juliet said firmly, and drew her down the hall to the kitchen.

"We didn't know how long you'd be, so I sent Mattie home to feed the grandchildren and take care of her daughter," Juliet said as she urged her mother to a chair. "But everything is nice and hot. I've kept the fire going in the stove ever since she left."

"Feels good, too." Dr. Laura dropped

into a chair and smiled as Juliet placed food before her. "I don't feel hungry — " She sniffed the fragrance from the plate and said eagerly, "That's not true. I'm starved."

"Then fall to, ma'am!" Juliet urged her, smiling, as she served her own plate, poured coffee for both of them and sat down opposite her mother.

"Everything go all right this afternoon?" Dr. Laura asked when she had taken the edge off her hunger. Instantly she apologized. "I'm sorry. That was tactless of me. Of course everything went all right. You were in charge."

Juliet laughed. "Phooey!" she mocked. "Don't try to wiggle out of it. You never leave me in charge of the clinic that you aren't worried for fear something will go wrong. I don't know just what could, unless we had some dire emergency. I always follow the things you've set down on the chart — "

Dr. Laura put out a hand and laid it on Juliet's.

"Darling, I *am* sorry. I didn't mean

to suggest that you couldn't cope with whatever might turn up!"

Juliet grinned at her fondly.

"Oh, be quiet, Doctor! Nurses are accustomed to being questioned about what happened while the doctor's back was turned," she mocked.

Dr. Laura grinned.

"Permit me to point out that doctors aren't accustomed to having nurses tell them to be quiet!" she reminded her.

Juliet grinned reminiscently.

"Oh, how often I have absolutely yearned to do just that!" she mourned mockingly.

Dr. Laura's eyes twinkled. "But remembered not to, I trust?"

"I graduated, didn't I?" Juliet retorted. "Does that answer your question?"

"Superbly, thank you!" And for no reason at all except that they were together, at the end of a tiring day, they both laughed.

2

JULIET struggled up from fathoms deep in sleep and listened groggily. Yes, there was somebody banging away on the front door, ignoring the side entrance, with its sign: "Clinic Entrance: Ring bell for Night Service."

She dragged herself out of bed, felt with her bare feet for her slippers and reached for the flannel dressing-gown that was always laid across the foot of her bed. As she opened her bedroom door into the big old-fashioned upstairs hall, she heard the pounding begin again. Somebody was obviously banging on the front door with clenched fists, and as she touched the light switch, her mother's door opened and Dr. Laura stood there, drawing on her own robe.

"Now what in the world — " she wondered.

"Stay put, honey. I'll see what it is;

maybe I can handle it, and you can get back to sleep," Juliet answered. She hurried down the wide stairs, belting her robe about her as she went, and turning on the light in the hall as she passed the switch beside the foot of the stairs.

She unlocked the big heavy front door, seldom used, since patients always used the side entrance. As she swung the door open, a man tumbled into the hall and fell flat on his face, mumbling something. At the foot of the drive, she heard a car start up and drive away.

She bent to the man, turned him on his back and was appalled at the condition of his bruised and battered face. He opened his eyes, looked up at her blearily, muttered, "Took you long enough to get here," and collapsed again.

Dr. Laura was hurrying down the stairs now, and as she reached the injured man, she caught her breath on a small gasp.

"What in heaven's name happened to him?" she asked.

Juliet looked down at the man. His city clothes were torn and mudstained, his shirt collar torn open, his hands bloody-knuckled and grimy.

"All he's been able to tell me so far is that it took me a long time to open the door," she answered. "As I did, I heard a car start up and drive away. He's evidently been worked over by some of the local people who don't like strangers prowling around Haleyville while the murder trial is going on."

Dr. Laura, examining the man where he lay, looked swiftly at Juliet in startled protest.

"Oh, you don't think the Haleyville people would do a thing like this!" she protested.

"I think the Crumps would," Juliet answered grimly.

"Oh, now, Julie, you don't know it was the Crumps," protested Dr. Laura, continuing her examination of the injured man.

"I think the Crumps would jump at the

chance to rid themselves of any stranger who endangers their illegal activities," Julie insisted.

"Well, he's badly bruised and beaten, but there are no broken bones." Dr. Laura forbore to argue further with Juliet.

The man opened his eyes and looked up at them groggily.

"Hey," be protested, "they told me they were taking me to a doctor."

"They did," Dr. Laura assured him briskly. "I'm Dr. Laura Cochran, and this is my daughter Juliet, a registered nurse."

The man's vision cleared and he managed to sit up, though the effort made him wince with pain.

"Well, what do you know!" he marveled. "A lady doc!"

Dr. Laura's gray eyes twinkled. "Well, a woman doctor, anyway," she mocked. "Now if you can get yourself into this wheelchair, Juliet and I will get you into bed."

"A wheelchair?" Obviously the man

was repelled by the thought. "Look, I'm not that beat up. Help me get on my feet, and I'll walk."

It was obviously a painful effort, but with the aid of the two women he managed it. But he could stagger only a few feet before he collapsed thankfully into the wheelchair that Juliet was holding steady for him.

"Hey, those guys were tougher than I thought." His tone tried to make light of his weakness.

"The Crumps are pretty tough," Juliet agreed.

He cocked his head and his eyes met hers, which were cool. "I suppose you know what happened, then?"

"We can guess, Juliet drawled. "Clearly you are a stranger here, because Dr. Laura and I know everybody in and around Haleyville, and we've never set eyes on you before. So you must be here in connection with that ugly murder trial that's been dumped on Haleyville's doorstep. The people are upset about it, and the Crumps are not people who take their dislike out just in talk, like other people here."

"Now, Julie — " protested Dr. Laura anxiously.

But the man was meeting Juliet's angry gray-green gaze.

"The fact that I'm not here because I wanted to be doesn't matter, I suppose?" he asked. "My paper sent me to cover the trial. Now that it's over, and the defendant has been sentenced, I had every intention of going back to Atlanta immediately. But when I called in my story, they said I could take my vacation now. And since I like this place, I decided to spend my two weeks here. Is that a crime?"

"I suppose not," Juliet answered reluctantly.

The man looked from one woman to the other and scowled, though the scowl brought a wince of pain to his sadly damaged features.

"Let's get him to bed, Julie. He needs rest and sleep," said Dr. Laura.

The man looked at her, startled.

"You're going to put me up here for the night?" he asked, and looked swiftly about the big old hall, with the white painted doors opening down the corridor.

"Why not? It's a hospital," answered Dr. Laura. She motioned to Juliet, who wheeled the chair across the corridor and into a large room that had once been the library, but which now held six beds and was the men's ward. "You should be quite all right in a few days."

"In a few days?" the man protested. "Hey, look, lady, I'm on my vacation!"

"Then aren't you lucky that you won't have to lose any time from your job?" Juliet mocked him. "We wouldn't have wanted you to miss reporting a single detail of the trial to your paper."

"Well, neither would the paper," the man said shortly.

As they reached the bedside, Juliet and Dr. Laura started to help him from the chair to the bed, but he thrust them away and growled, "I'm not a baby. I can make it under my own power," and practically fell into the bed.

Juliet had drawn off his mud-stained coat while he was in the hall, and now she started to unbutton his shirt. But once more he thrust her away.

"I said I could make it! I've been dressing and undressing myself since I was able to walk," he snapped at her. But some of the fire was gone from his tone. There were beads of sweat on his bruised and battered forehead, and his fingers that fumbled with the buttons of his shirt were clumsy.

Juliet thrust his hands away and said brusquely, "Oh, don't be an idiot. This is a hospital, and I'm a nurse. Now behave yourself."

Dr. Laura had gone across to the dispensary. As Juliet got the man's shirt off, she came back with a medication tray and began treating the bruised face and the scarred knuckles.

The man lay helplessly looking up at them. When Dr. Laura had finished and stood back, she smiled warmly at him.

"There, now, are you more comfortable?" she asked.

"Thanks, yes. You're very kind," the man muttered.

Dr. Laura smiled at him. "I'm a doctor, remember? And you're my patient."

Juliet stood on the other side of the bed, a chart in her hand, a ball-point pen poised.

"Now if you'll tell me your name and address and whom you'd like us to notify?" she suggested.

He scowled, and beneath the neat bandages Dr. Laura had applied, his eyes looked puzzled.

"Notify?" he repeated as though that had been the only word he had caught.

"Yes. Your family? Relatives?" Juliet was puzzled by his bewilderment.

"I don't have a family," he answered.

"You're not married?" Juliet asked.

"No," the man answered. "Are you?"

Juliet's gray-green eyes widened and her brows went up.

"No, but what's that got to do with anything at all?" she demanded.

"Oh, it's just something I like to know about very pretty girls I meet under interesting circumstances," he told her. And before she could answer that properly, he went on briskly, "I'm Steven Hayden of the *Atlanta Clarion,* and if you dare to notify anybody on the paper that I got beat up by some mountain moonshiners, I'll sue you for slander and anything else I can think of."

"We'd just like to know where the body should be shipped, in case that should be necessary," Juliet told him sweetly.

"Julie!" protested Dr. Laura sternly, shocked and distressed.

But Steve was meeting the cool, deliberate hostility in Julie's eyes without the slightest distress. In fact, there was a twinkle in his eyes, that were very brown beneath his thatch of red-brown hair.

"Oh, in case that happens, you can notify the paper, and I'm sure they will do whatever is necessary," he told Juliet blandly. "There is just one thing

I would like to ask of you, in case that does happen."

"Believe me, Mr. Hayden," protested Dr. Laura swiftly, deeply concerned about Juliet's callousness, "you are not seriously injured at all. Except for your face, which will take a while to heal, and some body bruises and contusions, you'll be quite all right within a week."

But Steve did not seem to be listening. His eyes had locked with Juliet's, and he was obviously waiting for her answer. .

"I don't promise I'll do it, whatever it is," Juliet told him frostily. "But you may as well ask. I can always say no."

"I bet you can and do, and have had a lot of practice saying it," Steve answered. "It's just a little something I have always heard that an R.N. does when one of her patients checks out of this mortal coil; she walks beside him to the mortuary. Will you do that for me?"

"It would be a pleasure," Juliet told him sharply, and went swiftly out of the room.

Steve looked up at Dr. Laura.

"What did I do to her to make her hate me?" he asked in honest bewilderment. "She doesn't even know me. How can you hate somebody you don't even know?"

"Julie loves Haleyville so much that the slightest thing that reflects against Haleyville she accepts as a deliberate insult to herself," Dr. Laura explained awkwardly. "Having this murder trial in Haleyville instead of in the county seat where it should have been, has upset her quite a bit. She resents the newspaper stories that will carry a Haleyville date line, because she says for years to come, when people think or hear the name, they will say, 'Oh, yes, wasn't that where that terrible murder took place?' They won't stop to realize that it was only the trial, not the murder, that took place here."

Steve was astounded.

"You mean she honestly thinks people will remember a two-bit murder trial like this one more than a few days?" he asked, and added hastily, "Oh, sure, I know it seemed earth-shaking to you people here. But with all the ugly things going on in the world, nobody will even think of it more than a day or two!"

Dr. Laura sighed and smiled at him.

"I hope you can convince Julie of that," she told him.

Steve looked thoughtful.

"I'm not sure that I want to," he said slowly. "A girl with that much devotion to her home town is a pretty rare creature. There must be more to Haleyville than I first thought if it can stir a girl like Juliet to such peaks of devotion."

"It's a pretty wonderful place, Mr. Hayden, to those of us who live here and who have spent our lives here, as Julie has. The only time she was away was when she was taking her nurse's training in Atlanta, and her service in emergency at the big charity hospital there seems to have given her a deep revulsion against big cities. I think she's secretly afraid something may happen to allow Haleyville to grow into a city, and she wants to stop it."

She stood up, checked his pulse and respiration and said briskly, "You must get to sleep now. The sedation is beginning to work, and I'm sure you'll feel much more like talking in the morning. This push-button beside your bed rings in my room and also in Julie's. So if you need us in the night, you have only to press it, and we'll come a-runnin'!"

"Thanks, Doctor. I repeat — you're very kind."

Her smile was warm and friendly.

"And I repeat, I'm a doctor and you are my patient," she answered as she moved toward the door. "Good night, Mr. Hayden."

Long after the door had closed behind her, and while he was unconsciously fighting off the drowsiness caused by the sedation, Steve went over and over the events that had brought him there to meet this girl, who seemed to him not only very pretty even in a bathrobe and hair curlers, but a most extraordinary girl in her devotion to her home town.

As he fell asleep, he had made up his mind that his vacation in Haleyville was going to be a working vacation and he was going to find out a lot that would make good copy for his paper, whether a certain green-eyed, black-haired young registered nurse liked it or not.

3

DR. LAURA looked up from the stove where she was turning crisping bacon and smiled lovingly as Juliet came in, very crisp and efficient-looking in an immaculate uniform, her cherished cap perched demurely on her shining blue-black hair.

"Good morning, darling," Dr. Laura said. And then, as she saw the uniform, "But aren't you going to church this morning? It's your turn, you know. I went last Sunday."

"I know, but somehow, I am not quite in the mood," Juliet answered. "I'll stay home and look after the patient and handle any emergencies, and you go. I stopped in to look at the patient, and he's sleeping the sleep of the just. So I'll give him his breakfast later."

Dr. Laura broke eggs into a yellow bowl, beat them briskly before pouring them into the hot pan, and eased the coffeepot back so it would not boil too fiercely.

"He seems like a rather likable chap, doesn't he?" Dr. Laura asked as she brought the plates to the table and accepted the toast that had obligingly popped up from the toaster beside Juliet's plate.

"Likable? The man who's going to turn Haleyville upside down and bring in a whole raft of summer visitors and hunters and fishermen and disturb the blessed peace and quiet of the place?" Juliet flared.

"Now, Juliet, you're being very unreasonable. Haleyville could stand some new blood," began Dr. Laura.

"Now, Mother, you haven't the faintest idea what you're talking about," Juliet said. "If you'd spent three years in a big charity hospital in Atlanta, serving most of the last year in Emergency you'd know more about the horrible, hideous things people in big cities are capable of doing to each other."

"Julie, I do wish it had been possible for you to take your training somewhere else," pleaded her mother. "And remember, your father and I interned at that same hospital — "

"That was twenty-eight years ago, Mother. And believe me, things have changed there."

"Well, I should hope so!" Dr. Laura said quickly. "Now eat your breakfast before it gets cold. If I'm going to church, I may as well get there in time for Sunday School. And if I run into Grady, I'll bring him home for lunch. Shall I?"

"Why not? I'll put an extra cup of water in the soup," Juliet agreed dryly.

"I imagine Grady's been very busy watching the trial these two weeks," said Dr. Laura.

"Oh, sure, Grady's had himself a postgraduate course in law, sitting there soaking up all the shenanigans of the big city lawyers that he can't find in his law books."

There was more than an edge of

disdain in Juliet's voice, and Dr. Laura eyed her anxiously.

"Well, that's only natural, honey," she pointed out. "Grady is ambitious. He wants to be a very fine lawyer, and he's as devoted to Haleyville as you are."

"He wants to go into politics, and he feels that being born and brought up in a hick town like Haleyville will do him no harm at all with the voters, once he can persuade the machine politicians to give him a chance at an elective office. And once he gets that chance, he's going to do everything he can to change Haleyville, first by getting a good road to the county seat and then, no doubt, by getting a hospital over here, which will make the clinic of no value whatever."

Dr. Laura eyed her with a sternness Juliet had seldom seen in her mother's eyes.

"I don't know what's gotten into you lately, Juliet," she said quietly. "Ever since we knew about the change of venue that was going to bring that man here for trial, you have been as

51

prickly as a porcupine. After all, Juliet, I can't thing of anything that would be better for Haleyville than some good roads, and I'd be the first to stand on Miss Sarah's front porch and cry aloud my great joy at having a hospital here. And as for the clinic, it was never more than a makeshift one, as you very well know. And I'll hear no more from you about wanting Haleyville to stand still and wither on the vine, like so many small, isolated towns have done."

"Yessum, Doctor, ma'am," said Juliet meekly.

Dr. Laura grinned at her forgivingly.

"Sure you don't mind taking extra duty today when it's really your turn to go to church and have the morning off?" she asked.

"Would I have suggested it if I did?" Juliet buttered some toast.

Dr. Laura eyed her warily.

"Promise you won't argue with the patient while I'm gone?"

Juliet's brows went up in elaborate and unconvincing surprise.

"Do I ever?" she asked innocently.

"Don't you always, given the slightest chance?"

Juliet shrugged. "Well, there's really not much point in arguing with this one. He'll be leaving as soon as he can drive, and that's the last we'll ever see of him. Whatever damage his stories about Haleyville can do has already been done, so what's the use of arguing with him?"

Dr. Laura nodded.

"That's a sensible attitude," she said with frank relief.

"Well, thanks, ma'am." Juliet smiled at her.

"Well, if I'm going to church, I'd better start getting ready." Dr. Laura rose from the table. "I'll help you clear the table. Want me to give the patient his breakfast?"

"I'll do that. You run along. He'll have to have his bath, and when I've done that I'll feed him," Juliet promised briskly.

"And no arguing?"

"I promised, didn't I?"

"So you did!" Dr. Laura smiled and left the kitchen, and a moment later, Juliet heard her footsteps climbing the stairs.

She went along the hall to the ward and saw that Steve was awake.

She greeted him cheerfully, but her eyes were still cool.

"Good morning," she said. "I've come to give you your bath."

He glared up at her, shocked.

"To do *what?* he barked.

"To give you your bath, of course." Juliet smiled at him sweetly. "And then I'll bring your breakfast."

"My dear young woman," he exploded, "I'm perfectly capable of getting to the bathroom, and I assure you I've been bathing myself for years."

Juliet shrugged, dropped a toweling robe across the foot of the bed and said sweetly, "Suit yourself, of course. But there's one thing I'm sure you won't be able to do for yourself, for a few days, anyway."

"And may I ask what that is?" He was

still outraged and mildly wary.

"Shave yourself," Juliet told him. "If you'll look in the mirror, I'm sure you'll understand why."

She went out. As the door closed behind her, Steve struggled out of bed and moved slowly and awkwardly toward the open door of the bathroom.

When she came back a little later with his tray, he was standing at the big window at the end of the ward, looking out over the vista of mountains, the steep valley where the brawling mountain stream splashed its way toward the faraway sea. As she came into the room, he turned, his hands jammed into the pockets of the toweling robe.

"It is a beautiful spot, this Haleyville of yours," he told her.

"Isn't it?" she agreed, her tone quite neutral as she set the tray on a small table and drew a chair in front of it. "I hope your breakfast suits you?"

"It looks delicious. And even if it didn't, I'm hungry enough to eat 'most anything," he assured her as he sat down and drew the table closer. "I'm wondering how a very pretty girl like you could possibly be happy in a quiet little place like this."

"I couldn't possibly be happy anywhere else," she answered. "It's my home. I was born in this house. I grew up in Haleyville. The only time I've been away was during my three years in training, and I loathed every minute of it and couldn't get back fast enough."

Her black head with its crop of short, springy curls beneath the cherished cap tilted defiantly, and her gray-green eyes were hostile.

"Of course I couldn't expect a 'flatland furriner' like you to understand that. Being a big-city man, you'd find Haleyville very dull and boring. So naturally, the minute you can leave, you will."

"And I suppose that will be entirely satisfactory to you?"

The gray-green eyes held an additional ration of frost.

"More than satisfactory, Mr. Hayden!

You've done all the damage you can to Haleyville by your stories in the paper — "

"Now see here; you haven't even read my stories!" he protested.

"I can imagine what they are like," she assured him dryly. "You describe all the quaint backwoods characters you've seen and talked to; all the gruesome details of the murder; the backwoods judge who chewed tobacco and the moonshiners who resented your presence here."

"There was none of that in any of my stories," he cut in sharply. "I thought the judge a very fine old gentleman; and the 'backwoods characters,' as you call them and as I never did, were all upstanding citizens. I must admit none of them seemed overly friendly to a stranger."

"Oh, didn't you know? People like those in Haleyville are never friendly to strangers."

"Well, I'd heard it, but I never believed it."

"You should. It's quite true."

Steve considered that for a moment,

and then he nodded.

"Well, maybe in the next couple of weeks, I can convince 'em my intentions are friendly," he mused aloud.

Juliet caught her breath, and her eyes flew wide.

Puzzled by her attitude, he said, "Why not, I've got a couple of weeks of vacation time on my hands, and I'm going to spend it here, exploring the area, doing some human interest stories about the people, perhaps including some of the patients of the clinic. Maybe I'll ride out with you on some of your morning calls."

"Oh, no, you're not!" she exploded wrathfully.

His brows went up in a puzzled scowl.

"My dear young woman — " he began.

"And don't you 'my dear young woman' me," Juliet cried hotly. "Oh, if you want to hang around Haleyville, there's nothing I can do to stop you. But riding out on my morning calls with me is something I can and will prevent! I will not have you invading the privacy of my patients!"

Neither of them had realized that Dr. Laura, dressed, hatted and gloved for church had come to the door and was looking at them in astonishment.

"What in the world are you two quarreling about?" she demanded, giving Juliet an admonishing glance.

"Do you know what this creature is planning to do?" Juliet asked her sharply.

"Why, no, but I'm sure you're going to tell me," Dr. Laura answered.

"He's planning to stay on for his two weeks' vacation and write human interest stories about Haleyville and its people," Juliet burst out. "And he even expects me to let him ride out with me when I visit my morning patients on my rounds."

"Why, I think that would be a wonderful idea," said Dr. Laura, and smiled warmly at Steve. "Haleyville could use the publicity."

Juliet protested, outraged, "And you

think I'd let him?"

Dr. Laura eyed her with unexpected firmness.

"I can't see how you could stop him," she answered, "or why you should want to, for that matter."

Juliet gasped, "Ride with me on my rounds and talk to my patients and write them up for his paper? You think I'd allow that?"

"Well, no, you probably wouldn't," Dr. Laura said coolly. "But I would."

"Mother, you wouldn't!"

"Juliet, I would!" Dr. Laura turned to Steve and said pleasantly, "I am going to church, Mr. Hayden. Would you like me to stop in at the hotel and collect any of your luggage?"

"Well, thanks, that's very decent of you," Steve answered gratefully. "And tell Mrs. Jensen at the hotel to save my room for me. I'll be back as soon as I'm dismissed from here."

"And that will be just as soon as we can possibly get you out of here," Juliet assured him, and went out of the room.

Dr. Laura smiled apologetically at Steve.

"Try to forgive her rudeness, Mr. Hayden, won't you?" she pleaded. "I often wish she could have taken her training somewhere else than in a large city. In Atlanta, she saw so much of what human beings can do to each other that she came back here with a complex about keeping Haleyville free of what she calls 'invaders,' and what we in Haleyville call 'progress towards a better life.' She doesn't agree with us about that phrase, I am sure I needn't tell you."

"No, she makes her point pretty clear," Steve agreed ruefully.

There was a sound floating in the crisp, sweet morning air — the sound of church bells. Dr. Laura looked at her wristwatch and said, "If I'm going to be in time for Sunday School, I'll have to hurry. I'll see you at lunch, Mr. Hayden."

"Do you suppose by that time you could possibly make it 'Steve' instead of Mr. Hayden?" he asked as she turned toward the door and she sent him a smiling glance over her shoulder.

"Of course, if that's the way you want it," she answered.

"It is, and thanks a lot," said Steve as she went out. A moment later he heard the sound of the jeep as she backed it down the steep drive to the road.

When Juliet came back for his breakfast tray, she was pale and composed, but frosty hostility was still in her eyes. She picked up the tray without a word. As she turned toward the door, Steve rose and laid a restraining hand on her arm.

"Look, lady," his tone and the look in his brown eyes were pleading, "can't we start all over again? Forget that you hate me, because you don't know me well enough to hate me. It takes a little time, a little knowledge of the other guy, before you can build up a hate like the one you're harboring. I didn't come here to cover this murder trial because I wanted to, but because I was sent here."

"But you're staying because you want

to, and you're planning to write stories about the 'quaint characters' — "

"They are not quaint. They are interesting and fascinating. I feel the readers of my paper would like to know about them. Is that a crime?"

"Well, no, I suppose not. Only it might bring a lot of strangers here, and they'd like the place and want to stay."

"And wouldn't that be a good thing for the town?"

"No! It would spoil it."

"Spoil it for you, or for the others here? Did you ever stop to think that you are pretty selfish to want to keep your little Shangri La all to yourself? What about the young people who go away as soon as they are old enough to want jobs, and have to hunt them somewhere else because there are none here? A few industries brought in, a few facilities for summer visitors, a few words about the fabulous meals Mrs. Jensen serves at her place — and Haleyville would be right in the stream of progress."

"Which is exactly what I don't want!"

she flared furiously, her hands that held the tray shaking so that the dishes rattled.

"What *you* don't want. But what about what the others here want?" Steve asked quietly.

She was still for a moment, and then she lifted to his eyes that were no longer frosty-green but soft with a mist of tears.

"*Am* I being selfish to want Haleyville left the way I've always loved it?" she asked, her voice pleading with him for a denial.

"I think you are, Julie, and I think you really know it but won't admit it, even to yourself," he told her. And while his tone was gentle, it was also implacable.

Juliet met his eyes for a long moment. Then she caught her breath on a small choked sound that was half a sob and went swiftly out of the room.

Steve dropped back into his chair and was surprised to realize, as he lit a cigarette, that his own hands were not quite steady.

4

IN Haleyville, the midday meal was always dinner. Thus, when Dr. Laura and Grady Alden arrived from church, dinner was almost ready. Juliet, flushed from her activities, looked up with a smile as Grady followed her mother into the kitchen.

"Hi!" he greeted her, his long, bony face alight with an eager smile. "Dr. Laura said it would be all right if I came home with her and split a sandwich with you. Then I could take you to dinner at the hotel tonight."

"Sorry, pal. Fresh out of sandwiches," Juliet informed him. "If you can make do with fried chicken, hot biscuits, creamy gravy, and a couple of vegetables, a salad and hot apple pie — "

Grady's groan was one of active appreciation.

"Make do, the woman says! For a

fellow that eats his own cooking three times a day, that's nectar for the gods!"

Juliet laughed. "Well, that's what you're going to get," she told him. "How was church?"

Dr. Laura's brows went up.

"Why, what a question! Preacher Cecil was in fine voice, and his sermon was excellent. The choir sang slightly off key. Mary Judson sang the solo and forgot the words. She was too vain to wear her glasses, so she couldn't look at her music. I'd say it was about the same as usual. But just the same, it was an illuminating experience."

"Because you saw so many of your old friends, I'm sure," Juliet teased her, and added, "Since our patient is able to be up and about, should we let him come to the table and eat with us? Or do you suppose he'd like a tray?"

"I think he'd like to join us at the table," Dr. Laura said firmly. "Grady wants to meet him."

Juliet slipped a second pan of biscuits into the oven and straightened, eying

Grady without favor.

"Why?" she demanded.

"Why?" Grady looked puzzled. "Why, because he's from out of town, and he's a newspaperman. Never underestimate the power of the press, Julie my girl."

"Provided you're ambitious to be in politics. As for me, I've seen all the newspaper people I care to see, thanks a whole lot!" Her voice was curt.

Dr. Laura sighed and said, "Grady, don't try to argue with her. She's obsessed. Come along, and I'll introduce you to Steve."

"Oh," said Juliet, "so now he's Steve, is he?"

Dr. Laura glanced back over her shoulder.

"It's the way he wants it," she answered coolly.

"Shall I set the table in the dining room? Perhaps Steve wouldn't like eating in the kitchen," Julie suggested dryly.

"Well, since it's been quite a few years since we had a dining room, and we needed an examination room much worse and made the dining room into one, I'm afraid Steve will have to like eating in the kitchen."

Juliet nodded. "Well, hurry it up. The biscuits will be done by the time you and Steve get dressed! I know you refuse to do anything but go to church in your best clothes."

"Well, of course, since they're my 'go-to-meetin' clothes,'" Dr. Laura quoted one of Mattie's favorite phrases. But as she went out into the corridor, her eyes were troubled.

A little later, Steve and Grady came into the kitchen, and Steve looked in frank delight at the big, old-fashioned kitchen with its row of blossoming plants on the window-sills, framed by crisp red and white check gingham curtains that matched the cloth covering the table set in the center of the room. On it Juliet was placing platters heaped with savory-smelling food.

"A real old-fashioned kitchen!" he said in obvious delight. "I'd forgotten that such kitchens existed. I thought nowadays they were all just tiny closets that could be hidden if you closed a door. All this one needs is a big gray and white cat asleep on the hearth."

Dr. Laura laughed as she indicated his chair.

"Well, Junior is out in the barn sleeping off his night ramble," she answered gaily.

"Oh, you do have a cat?" asked Steve.

"Well, of course. What country kitchen wouldn't have, even if he does prefer to sleep in the barn?" Dr. Laura asked.

"I'd like to meet him."

Juliet looked at him swiftly.

"Do you like cats?" she asked.

Steve looked surprised. "Well, who doesn't?"

Grady grinned wryly. "I don't, for one. Julie and I don't quarrel about anything else. I can't stand cats. I prefer dogs. Cats are so tricky, so deceiving. One minute they purr against your leg, and the next minute they sharpen their claws in you."

"But that's because Junior knows you don't like him, and he wants you to know he's not trying to curry favor with you," Juliet told him cheerfully. Her smile at Grady was so warm that Steve stared at her in surprise, because he had not known that she could be so friendly. But when her eyes met his it was as though a curtain had come down over her face, wiping out the warmth and friendliness.

Truly, he told himself grimly as the meal progressed, here was a girl who had been badly hurt sometime, undoubtedly during the years she had spent in Atlanta; and he would have liked very much to know how.

Grady made some comment about an article in the Sunday paper, and Steve said, "Oh, yes, that's something I've been wondering about. How do you manage to get the paper here on Sunday? I'd think it would take a day or so for the mail edition to reach you."

Juliet answered before Grady could, and there was a flash in her gray-green eyes that all but made Steve flinch.

"Are you surprised to find there are people in Haleyville who can or want to read the Sunday papers?" she drawled.

"Well, in view of your resentment of the invasion of an innocent and law-abiding representative of one of the Atlanta papers, I'm a little surprised that you don't refuse to allow the papers even to enter your cherished Shangri La," Steve told her, and could not keep the edge out of his voice.

"Oh, we aren't that narrow-minded," she mocked him. "We like to read about the hideous things that happen in big cities, and then we can be all the happier in our Shangri La, as you choose to call it."

"But you still haven't told me how you manage to get the Sunday papers here the same day they are on the streets in Atlanta," he reminded her, his jaw setting a little at the insolence in her tone.

Dr. Laura and Grady exchanged uneasy glances but Steve and Juliet were studying each other like the sworn enemies they were and seemed completely unaware of the other two.

"Oh, the papers come up in the train to the county seat, and Jed Holcomb drives over in his jeep and picks up a dozen or more for the people here who want to realize just how fortunate they are to live here instead of in a city," Juliet told him. "And if you're wondering if we can read and write up here, we have an excellent school — "

"One room, in an old place that used to be a barn. And class is conducted by a retired schoolteacher who came to the mountains looking for a place where she might be needed and found it in Haleyville," Grady cut in. Now there was a faint edge in his voice, too, and a warning look in the eyes that he fastened on Juliet. "There are twenty-two children in the school this year, all, of course, in the elementary grades. When they finish with Miss Letty, they will enter the consolidated high school at the county line next fall."

"Miss Letty sounds like an ideal

candidate for my first human interest story," said Steve happily.

Grady asked swiftly, "Oh, you're staying on to do some human interest stories?"

"I'm on vacation, and I decided Haleyville would be an ideal place to spend a vacation. The people interest me a lot — " Steve began.

Juliet cut in, "Like circus freaks, perhaps?"

"Nothing of the sort," Steve answered sharply. "You must admit that to city people, Haleyville citizens, self-reliant, self-sufficient and independent, would be fascinating copy."

"I'm sure of it." Juliet's tone was cutting, though her voice was not quite steady and there was a mist of angry tears in her eyes. "But they won't talk to you. You needn't count on that. We're wary of strangers up here."

Steve touched his bruised and battered face with a finger and nodded.

"I have proof of that," he drawled. "But now that the trial is over, and the resultant ugliness swept away from your charming little village, I hoped that people would soften up a bit."

"Well, they won't, you can be sure of that." Juliet flung the words at him hotly.

Dr. Laura said sternly, "Juliet, behave yourself. Mr. Hayden is not only our patient; he's a guest beneath our roof."

"And don't ever underestimate the power of the press, Julie." Grady smiled in an effort to ease the tension, that was growing by the second.

"Oh, for a man who's ambitious to get into politics, perhaps the power of the press is important," Juliet snapped.

Steve turned to Grady, secretly relieved that the impending argument with this extraordinary girl was at least being postponed.

"Oh, you're interested in politics?" he asked.

Grady grinned wryly, and a trace of color showed on his lean, bony face.

"What small town lawyer isn't, nowadays?" he answered dryly. "Of course I don't suppose I have a chance of winning without the support of the county machine, and they're not too likely to pick a fellow from a town as small as Haleyville and set back in the mountains like this."

"Well, it didn't hurt Lincoln any to come from a small town and be what they called a 'backwoods lawyer'," Steve told him, and added in all sincerity, "Do you mind if I say you bear a striking resemblance to early pictures I've seen of the 'young Lincoln'?"

Frankly pleased, Grady answered, "Why, no. In fact, I'd be quite flattered."

Juliet burst out, "Grady, don't be a fool. Can't you see he's making fun of you?"

Steve turned on her, scowling and angry, his eyes blazing.

"That's not true! Ye gods, what an unpleasant creature you are! Dr. Laura, I'm afraid you didn't spank her often enough when she was growing up."

Dr. Laura eyed Juliet with cool disfavor.

"I'm afraid you're quite right, Steve. In addition, she tended to get quite a bit out of hand during the three years she was away. I scarcely knew her when she came back. She didn't come home during vacations, and three years is a long time."

Juliet stood up, and her chin was tilted at a defiant angle as she looked from one to the other.

"I'm sorry you three find me so difficult to get along with, but since you do and make it so plain, I'll go wake Junior up and feed him while you finish your dinner," she told him, her voice shaking. Then she turned and went out of the back door, and they saw her running down the path toward the barn.

Dr. Laura said uncomfortably, "I'm so sorry, Steve. I can't think what got into her."

Steve grinned ruefully.

"I can. She's made it very plain from the beginning that she does not want an invasion from the outside world to come to Haleyville, and she is afraid that what I am planning to write for my paper might accomplish just that," he answered. "I'm afraid she's flattering me and the power of the press you were kind enough to mention, Grady."

"Well, I sincerely hope it will bring in some outside people," Grady told him firmly. "That's what we need here: new blood; new industry. Not that we have any old industries, come to think of it. From my viewpoint, it would be good to have an industry in which the local people could earn a living, so they would not have practically to starve trying to farm their perpendicular acres! Of course at present we don't have any facilities for taking care of summer visitors. But we could build them, and that would provide some jobs. And jobs are desperately needed. Of course we'd have to have a good road, one that could be negotiated by something other than a mule or a jeep, before we could hope to get people to come here."

Steve grinned at him, liking the man and making no effort to hide the fact.

"That would be a good campaign

platform for you, Grady. Get the people interested and win votes. I'm sure that if you did get elected, you'd do everything possible to carry out your promises."

"Thanks," said Grady gratefully. "Of course, my only hope would be a seat on the county commission to begin with. But if I could win that, it would be a start."

He stood up and said, "It was a mighty fine dinner, Dr. Laura. Thanks for inviting me. I'll go out now and see if I can help Julie wake up Junior. He sleeps pretty soundly after one of his night rambles, but the sound of my voice should do it. He hates me so that I think he even growls at me in his sleep."

"Oh, it's not quite that bad, Grady." Dr. Laura laughed. "I think it's chiefly that he smells the scent of your dog, and of course dogs are his natural enemies."

"Don't hint that he's afraid of dogs," Grady warned her with a grin. "Junior's afraid of nothing on four legs or two!"

"He sounds like quite a cat. I can't wait to meet him," Steve said. Grady made a little gesture and went out of the kitchen and down the path Juliet had followed.

The big old barn was flooded with sunlight through its many cracks and broken boards. The smell was faintly musty, since it hadn't been used as a barn in many years. But it was a pleasant place, Grady felt, as he entered it and paused to adjust his eyes to the gloom of a big stall where there was a feed box, well off the floor and padded with an old blanket, which he knew to be Junior's favorite sleeping place. The feed box was empty, and so Grady walked on down the middle of the barn and out at the far end.

Juliet sat on a big flat rock on a steep slope that descended sharply to the valley below. Her back was to the barn, and the big gray and white cat lay peacefully beside her. As Grady spoke the cat rose, growled and hissed at him and leaped away into waist-high grass and weeds.

"Oh, it's you," said Juliet as she

glanced at him over her shoulder.

"Didn't Junior tell you that?" Grady grinned as he approached. "Shall I go away?"

"Why? There's room for two here. It's quite a big rock." Juliet moved slightly and made room for him. "How's our self-elected denizen of the press who's going to bring civilization — you should excuse the expression — to our benighted backwoods jungle?"

"Oh, he's helping Dr. Laura with the dishes, and they are having a marvelous time," Grady answered, matching his tone to hers. "I *do* think you were a bit rough on him, Julie."

"And he's not going to be rough on Haleyville?"

"Of course not. He thinks it's a wonderful little place or he wouldn't want to spend his vacation here."

"A vacation? Did you know he expects to ride with me on my rounds and do stories about some of my patients?" she demanded.

"Why, no, I hadn't heard that!"

"And Dr. Laura's going to *let* him!"

Grady was silent for a moment, and then he asked gently, "Well, Julie, would that be so terrible? After all, some of your patients might be delighted. They might like having their pictures in the paper in a city as far away as Atlanta."

"Do you think Miss Letty will let him do a story about her?"

"I think she'd be delighted, because it will point up the need for a real school in Haleyville — "

"And you don't think hers is?"

"I think she does a wonderful job with what she has to work with, but I'm sure she'd be overjoyed if the kids could have better supplies and more of them."

Before she could speak, he put his arm about her shoulders and drew her close, resting his lean, bony cheek against her dark curls. He said softly, "Honey, we both know how we feel about newcomers to Haleyville; we're on opposite sides about that. But does it have to make us enemies?"

"No, of course not, Grady, I'm just

selfish, I suppose," she admitted ruefully.

Grady raised his head and stared at her.

"Selfish?" he repeated as though he had not the faintest idea of her meaning. "You selfish? Now that's about the most absurd thing I ever heard!"

"Steve Hayden thinks I am."

"Oh, he does, does he? Remind me to punch him in the nose the next time I see him."

Juliet managed a feeble smile.

"Oh, you wouldn't want to do that, Grady. Remember he's a newspaperman, and we mustn't ever underestimate the power of the press," she reminded him dryly.

"Well, I suppose not," he agreed reluctantly. "You know why I want to get into politics, don't you, darling?"

"Of course. So you can bring progress to Haleyville, whether Haleyville wants it or not."

"That's not it at all, and you know it. I want to get into politics so I can ask you to marry me and be able to offer you something faintly approaching a decent life," he told her with such unexpected vigor that she stared up at him, startled.

"Why, Grady."

He pretended to glare at her.

"Now don't go all coy and maidenly on me, girl," he ordered her. "What else have we had in mind since I first started carrying your books to school when we were kids!"

"Well, you've never come right out and said it before!"

"Why should I? I thought it was understood between us!"

He was frankly puzzled, and his brows were drawn into a scowl.

"Understood?" Juliet laughed aloud. "Oh, Grady, darling. You're a very smart lawyer, but you don't know beans about women."

"Of course not," Grady admitted without embarrassment. "I never claimed to. But are women a race apart? I mean, don't they take a few things for granted? Don't they accept understandings and plan ahead the way men do?"

Juliet's laughter was quick and warm. "My darling goof!" She laughed. "And you *are* a goof to think that the woman has yet been born who will just slide into an engagement with a man for no other reason than that they have been going together since the Year One! Every woman alive wants a moment that she can hold close and warm in her heart's memories until she is old and white-haired and senile. And she expects the man she loves to give her that moment to remember always.

Grady looked down into her uplifted face, and there was a faint trace of uneasiness in his eyes as he said cautiously, "I'm almost afraid to ask. I'm pretty stupid about women. You said so yourself. What moment to remember are you talking about?"

Juliet laughed, a soft, silvery laugh.

"The moment when a man she loves come boldly and bravely out with the words, 'My darling, I love you. Will you marry me?' Or words to that effect."

"Oh," said Grady with such frank relief that Juliet's eyes danced, "is that all? Well, I was planning to say those words just the minute I could see some prospect I'd be able to take proper care of you."

Juliet lifted her head, and her eyes were dancing, though her expression tried very hard to be stern.

"Oh, you're that sure that the answer from me will be 'yes'?" she mocked him.

Grady's arm tightened about her and drew her close against him.

"Well, it had just better be!" he warned her. And though he tried to sound ominous, even threatening, the tenderness in his voice and the warmth of his embrace were gentle and ardent.

For a long moment Juliet was still within the circle of his arm, and then she stirred restlessly and freed herself and turned to look at him.

"Some day, Grady, perhaps," she said at last.

Grady scowled. "Some day?" he repeated.

She smiled faintly. "Well, you said yourself that when you were able to support me in unimagined luxury, luxury I never imagined anyway, you'd break down and offer to share your wealth with me," she mocked him. "And we both know that day hasn't come yet. But perhaps some day — "

His jaw set, and he turned a sombre gaze out over the lovely sweep of mountains and valleys and nodded.

"Well, it's not going to be too long, darling," he promised her. "You can definitely count on that."

Juliet studied him curiously for a moment.

"Mind if I point out something?" she asked.

He looked down at her warily.

"That all depends on what it is," he answered.

"It's just that when a girl is in love and wants to be married, she doesn't care a darn whether she's marrying a man who is rolling in wealth or whether he hasn't two cents to rub together in his pockets," she told him. "The only thing she's concerned about is whether or not he loves her and wants to marry her."

"Well, that's something you needn't worry about," Grady assured her. "You know you're the only girl I've ever wanted to marry or even dated. But I would like to have a decent roof over your head before I ask you."

"Your house is nice and snug."

"The kitchen roof leaks like a sieve, and the front part of the house is my office. Usually there are two or three very uneasy clients hanging around in what used to be the living room, waiting for me to finish with the one in my so called private office," he reminded her.

Her brows went up in an elaborate pretense of surprise.

"You sound like a very busy man," she drawled, "With so many clients — "

"Whose fees are usually paid in a couple of plump, freshly dressed chickens, or a home-cured ham, or even a barrel of molasses. A fellow could get rich with such clients," he informed her ruefully.

Juliet nodded in complete understanding.

"I know Haleyville's barter system very well," she answered. "Dr. Laura and I use it a lot. But then such fees are edible and save grocery bills."

He looked at her uneasily, scowling a little, and Juliet went on hastily, "Oh, I'm not trying to talk you into any thing you don't want to do, like for instance marrying me this very minute — "

"And you know darned well nothing in the world would make me happier," he cut in swiftly. "It's just that I won't let you in for any such life. It isn't good enough for you. You deserve something so much better."

Juliet smiled at him and patted his cheek lightly.

"You're sweet, Grady dear, and one of these days when you are a 'big shot' politician, we'll talk about it again. But now I'd better go in and see if Dr. Laura needs me. I walked out on the clearing up after dinner, and if somebody came in with an urgent call for help, she'd be overwhelmed."

"Which, permit me to point out, is something I can't imagine Dr. Laura ever being," Grady answered as he drew her to her feet and, with an arm about her, walked with her through the dim, musty-smelling old barn out into the brilliant sunlight that spilled through the tall pines which dotted the wide, ragged back lawn.

"She is pretty wonderful, isn't she?" Juliet asked, turning her head to smile up at him.

"Getting you as my wife is the dream of my life," Grady assured her. "And a fantastic extra bonus will be to get Dr. Laura as a mother-in-law. I can't imagine any man having greater luck!"

Juliet laughed. "Are you quite sure you aren't even more anxious to win Dr. Laura than you are to woo me?" she mocked him.

He paused on the path and looked

down at her, his arm tightening about her.

"I am more anxious to marry you, darling, than I am of some day to be governor of the state!" he told her with such deep sincerity that she felt tears spring to her eyes, even as she smiled at him.

"Well, some day, darling, you may have both the governor's mansion and me," she told him gently.

As they came into the kitchen Dr. Laura turned from the big old-fashioned sink and smiled fondly at them.

"You timed it exactly right," she informed them. "The last dish has just been washed and put away, and I'm washing out the tea towels. Ten minutes earlier, there might have been work for you to do."

Juliet laughed. "Oh, we're smart, we are! We knew better than to come back any earlier."

"Steve dried the dishes as I washed them." Dr. Laura smiled over her shoulder at Steve, who was very carefully placing a dish in the cabinet.

"And I only broke one cup," Steve boasted happily.

Juliet's brows went up in mock surprise.

"Well, aren't you the clever one?" she mocked him.

"I told him it didn't matter, because we have more cups than we ever use," Dr. Laura comforted Steve.

Steve was studying Juliet curiously.

"I heard a very odd sound just then," he told her.

"Did you? Such as what?" Juliet asked.

"It was a laugh, a gay, young, girlish sort of laugh. I wondered if it could possibly have been you that laughed."

Juliet said stiffly, "I frequently laugh when I find anything to laugh about."

"And of course up here there isn't very much that's funny, is there?" Steve asked quietly.

A small fan of carnation color touched her cheeks, and her eyes went frosty.

"I have never found Haleyville so dull," she told him. "We have a lot of fun here. But of course it wouldn't be the kind of fun that would appeal to a 'flat-land furriner'."

Steve looked at Dr. Laura in frank appeal.

"She's slugging me again," he complained.

"I know, and she's too big to be spanked," Dr. Laura replied, eying Juliet with a look of frank annoyance. "I can't think what's gotten into her lately. She has always been a rather pleasant, even friendly child, but nowadays — " She sighed and lifted her shoulders in a slight shrug and spread her hands, palm upward, in a gesture that acknowledged her helplessness to cope with the problem.

Juliet said stiffly, "You both know perfectly well what's gotten into me these last few days, and we aren't going to discuss it any more, at least not now. Grady and I have some news for you, Mother."

Dr. Laura looked from one to the other expectantly, and did not miss the fact that Grady's glance at Juliet was startled and faintly uneasy. But it was Steve at whom Juliet looked when she delivered her news, and there was a faint hint of defiance in her voice.

"Grady and I are going to be married," Juliet announced.

Dr. Laura made a grimace as she turned to put down the freshly rinsed tea towel in a small pan.

"So what else is new?" she asked lightly, and picked up the pan, preparatory to hanging the tea towels out in the sunshine.

Juliet blinked. "Is that all you have to say?" she demanded.

Dr. Laura eyed her with an amused twinkle in her eyes.

"Were you expecting me to be surprised?" she mocked. "I've been expecting to hear that since you were children. "Have you selected a date?"

Grady said hastily, "Oh, she doesn't mean right away. It'll be when I'm in a position to take decent care of her."

Steve, leaning against the wall, his arms folded, was watching Juliet's averted face. Dr. Laura smiled at Grady and pretended to sigh.

"And here I was thinking you were going to take her off my hands right away," she mourned.

"Ha!" Juliet sniffed. "If he did, who'd make the morning rounds for you?"

"Oh, you'd still have time for that, even as the wife of a young and upcoming attorney." Dr. Laura smiled at her. "You wouldn't give up nursing, that I know. And your beloved patients on your morning rounds would probably shoot Grady if he married you and took you away."

She picked up the pan and started toward the kitchen door. Juliet took the pan from her and said, "Here; let me hang them out."

She went out of the kitchen and down across the old porch to the path that led down to a clothesline hung between two big trees, leafless now in the early spring sunshine. She had just hung the last towel and picked up the pan to return to the house when Steve stood before her.

"I got your message," he told her quietly.

Startled, she repeated, "What message?"

"Yours and Grady's," he answered. "You were warning me not to fall in love with you."

Juliet caught her breath, and color crept into her cheeks.

"Don't be ridiculous!" she snapped. "As if you could or would!"

Steve was studying her with a curious, completely grave scrutiny.

"I wish I could think it was ridiculous, but I'm afraid I can't," he told her, and there was a hint of grimness in his voice. "I really like Grady."

"I'm sure he'd be very happy to know that." Her voice was edged with anger.

"Oh, he knows it," Steve assured her. "He's quite a fellow, and his political ambitions make sense."

"How kind of you to say so." Her voice made it very nearly a sneer.

"So you can see how much I hate the thought of upsetting his hopes of marrying you."

Juliet caught her breath on a little outraged gasp. "As if you could!" she snapped.

"Oh, I don't know. I can be pretty stubborn once I've set my mind on acquiring something I want very badly."

"You really are absurd, Mr. Hayden!" she snapped. "There's one thing I think you may have overlooked. I know it bothers you to be up here among the freaks and zanies, and know how bored you must be. But you should realize that we mountain girls don't fall for smooth lines like your city gal friends."

"That's one of the many things I like about mountain girls like you, Julie. You aren't easily bowled over, by a fancy line." He seemed undisturbed by her jibe. "Its one of many, many things I find so very attractive about you. Shall I tell you what some of the others are?"

"Please don't bother."

"Oh, it's no bother. It's just that I'm afraid we haven't time now, because it would take me quite a while. But I'll be here for a couple of weeks — "

"You are planning to stay, then, in spite of everything?"

He grinned at her disarmingly.

"Let's say I'm planning to stay because of everything, and chiefly because of you."

"Then let me tell you here and now, Mr. Steve Hayden, that it won't do you a bit of good," she protested. "I've always planned to marry Grady, just as Grady has always planned to marry me. And there is no possible chance that either of us will change our mind."

"Don't be too sure about that." Steve was quite calm, quite good-tempered, but, she realized, also quite determined. "A lot can happen in a couple of weeks. And then there are weekends. The drive up here isn't bad at all, except for the road between here and the county seat. And who knows? That may be improved before the summer is over."

Juliet stared at him and smothered a childish and all but irresistible impulse to smack him with the dish pan she was still holding.

"I suppose you think you can get the road improved?" she asked with biting sarcasm.

"I think Grady and I, by working together and getting some of the local citizens interested, may be able to do something about it," he said quite frankly. "After all, Grady's politically ambitious, and what would do his ambitions more good than getting a better road in the area?"

She set her teeth against the bitter words that rose. But she had already made her position on the matter of preserving Haleyville's quiet and isolation so plain that further words were a waste of breath.

"Julie, stop fighting me," he pleaded so unexpectedly that she had the feeling of taking a step in the dark and plunging down a flight of steps she hadn't known were there.

"Fighting you?" she gasped shakily.

"You have been, from the very first moment I set eyes on you," he reminded her in that quiet, deeply vibrant, pleading voice. "Oh, I know you resented my being sent here. We've been all over that. But can't you forget why I came, and just realize that I am here and be a little kind to me?"

"A little kind?" she stammered inanely.

For the flicker of an instant a smile tugged at the corners of his mouth, then was gone before she could be certain that it had been there.

"I'll settle for that as a beginning," he assured her. "Later, when we've become better friends, perhaps we can achieve something a little warmer. Because eventually, Julie, you are going to love me."

Julie gasped, "Why — you — you — "

"Just as I am quite sure that I'm going to love you, given the faintest possible chance," he said quite firmly.

Her eyes blazed and her color was high. But back of the outrage in her eyes there was a faint uneasiness, as though for the first time she was not quite sure just how to answer him.

"That's why I said I'm sorry I like

Grady," he said as though he felt a need to explain his position. "I'd much rather take a girl away from a man I disliked — "

"And you think you can take me away from Grady?" she asked.

His jaw set hard and his eyes were stern.

"I'm certainly going to try my darnedest to do just that!"

As Juliet met his level gaze, her color burned deeply. And within her she could feel the hard, uneven thudding of her heart, like the galloping hooves of a runaway horse.

"You really are the most absurd creature I've ever had the misfortune to meet," she said inadequately, turned and went running back to the house.

Steve stood where she had left him and made no effort to follow her. As she went through the kitchen door, she glanced over her shoulder and saw him still standing there, his back to the house now, his hands jammed deep into his pockets as though he were merely enjoying the breath-taking view.

Juliet went on into the house, let the screen door slam behind her and stood for a long moment, her shaking hands pressed over her hot face, helplessly listening to the crazy clamor of her heart.

5

FOR the next few days, Juliet went her accustomed way. Steve had gone back to the hotel on Monday, his bruised and battered face healing well, the contusions on his body practically vanished.

Wherever Juliet went on her rounds, and during afternoon and evening clinic hours, she heard about the 'city feller' that was writing up Haleyville and making friends wherever he went. He and Grady were all over the place, she heard, and Grady was introducing Steve as his friend, which wiped out any suspicion or aversion the local people might feel for a 'flat-land furriner'.

Now and then, when she came in from her rounds at noon, Steve would be waiting for her. He would help her to unload the jeep, and help the ambulatory patients she had picked up along the route into the clinic or to benches beneath the tall trees where they usually preferred to wait for Dr. Laura's services.

She had not been alone with him since that Sunday afternoon under the trees when he had made the utterly ridiculous statement that he was going to pursue her, that he was going to he a rival of Grady. She had been careful not to be alone with him. Occasionally he had given her a half-amused, half-exasperated glance, as though he were perfectly aware that she was avoiding him and also were quite aware of the reason.

One morning she was preparing to make her usual rounds among her patients back in the mountains, and was loading her supplies for the rounds in the jeep, when Dr. Laura came hurrying out to her.

"Steve called," Dr. Laura announced. "He's on his way. You may have to wait a few minutes for him."

Juliet stared at her.

"Why should I wait for him?" she demanded.

"Because he's riding with you on your rounds this morning."

Juliet gasped in outrage, "Oh, no he's not!"

"Oh, yes, he is," said Dr. Laura and met her eyes. "We are not going to argue about this, Julie. I have given him permission."

"But, Mother!"

"I said we are not going to argue, Julie," Dr. Laura answered her anguished protest. "That's an order, Nurse!"

Juliet stared at her with stunned eyes, meeting a steely, implacable look she had never before seen in her mother's eyes but that she had seen in the eyes of doctors at the hospital giving instructions and orders to nurses. It would no more have occurred to her to protest an order given by Dr. Laura than an order by one of the doctors at the hospital, but she was bitterly hurt and dazed that she should hear such an order from her mother. In that moment they were not mother and daughter, loving each other, devoted, happy together.

They were a doctor and a nurse, one giving orders, the other accepting them without question.

Juliet drew a long hard breath, and her eyes clung to her mother's, hoping against hope that there would be a softening there. But there was no hint of such a thing.

"I'm sorry to pull rank on you, Nurse," said Dr. Laura, still in the cool tone of one giving an order and expecting it to be obeyed instantly and without the slightest question. "But I feel the columns he is doing about us are quite valuable. And I insist that we give him every possible assistance."

Juliet was spared the necessity of making an answer by the arrival of Steve's car.

He parked beneath the shadow of a tall tree whose faintly green new leaves were just breaking into view, and came swiftly to the jeep, smiling a pleasant greeting at Dr. Laura and saying briskly to Juliet, "Sorry. I hope I didn't keep you waiting. Shall we get going?"

Juliet gave him a glance that should have shriveled him as she slid behind the wheel of the jeep and said through her teeth, "I had orders from the doctor to wait for you."

"Oh?" Steve smiled at Dr. Laura, whose anxious eyes were on Juliet. "Thanks a lot, Dr. Laura. I won't let you be sorry about this."

"I trust you won't, Steve!" Dr. Laura answered. Juliet, without so much as a glance at her mother, let the jeep roll down the drive and into the road.

As the jeep headed toward the end of the road, where it turned into little more than a mule track, Steve said quietly, "I hope you aren't too angry with me over this."

Juliet said through her teeth, her voice low and shaking, "I hate you!"

"I'm sorry about that," said Steve, although his tone held very little sorrow. "I felt this would give me material for one of the most important columns on the mountains. I knew you'd fight me, so I called Dr. Laura. She and Grady agreed it would make a very effective column; maybe several. I understand some of your patients are quite interesting characters."

"They are also human beings, entitled to some privacy and to some dignity," she burst out hotly.

"None of the others I've written about have been a bit upset," Steve pointed out quietly. "In fact, they were more than willing to talk and to have their pictures taken."

Juliet did not deign to answer him. Her attention was on the road ahead.

"D'you know," Steve observed after a long moment of silence, "I can't help wondering what happened to you in Atlanta to make you so publicity-shy."

Juliet swung him a hostile glance, her mouth a thin line.

"Are you trying to ask if I was jilted by some brash young intern; or maybe a staff doctor? If that's bothering you, please let me assure you nothing of the kind happened. I was much too busy for such foolishness as falling in love."

"Foolishness, she calls it." Steve

considered that for a moment, and his grin infuriated her. "That means there are an awful lot of fools loose in the world, then."

"There certainly are, and one of the biggest of them is sitting right here beside me," she told him savagely.

"Well, at least you won't forget about me when I'm gone," be drawled.

"I won't ever forget about you! You may definitely count on that!" she assured him.

"Good! That's what I wanted to know," he told her contentedly. "I'd much rather have you hate me furiously than just be indifferent."

"Then you should be as happy as a lark, for I certainly hate you plenty! And indifferent to you I could never be!" she flashed at him.

"That relieves my mind," he said with a cheefulness that made her long to do something violent. But she only went on driving until at last they came to a drab gray cabin that clung to the side of the mountain, thin blue smoke plunging above its stick-and-mud chimney.

"This is my first call," she told him, and lifted her worn black bag from the jeep. "I suppose you insist on going in with me?"

"Of course," said Steve, as though he considered the question silly. He followed her up the crooked path to the cabin, and up the broken steps to a door that swung open as they crossed the porch.

A slatternly-looking woman, a baby perched on her hip, two others clutching at her skirts, welcomed them. She greeted Juliet warmly but was obviously disconcerted at the sight of Steve.

"Hello, Mamie," said Juliet, and with a nod indicated Steve. "This is Mr. Hayden, from Atlanta. He writes for a newspaper down there."

Mamie smoothed back her flair, hitched the baby to a more comfortable spot on her hip and said, flurried and excited, "Why, yes, I reckon we been hearing about Mr. Hayden. Come on in. Don't notice the house. It's a mess, Maw being in bed and the young-'uns running wild."

Steve accepted the introduction with pleasant courtesy as Juliet brushed past Mamie into the room at the left which was the cabin's main living room. In a vast old-fashioned bed in a corner lay an old woman who was so tiny and so much a bag of bones that she barely lifted the heavy covers that were spread over her. Though a log fire blazed in the fireplace and the room felt uncomfortably hot to Juliet and Steve, the old woman was huddled beneath the covers, shaking. She wore a bonnet-shaped nightcap, and as she turned her head fretfully on the pillow and looked at Juliet, her thin voice rose in a complaint.

"You're late, Miss Julie. I thought maybe you'd forgot about me," she whined.

"Now, Grandma, you know I wouldn't ever forget about you," Juliet told her soothingly as she lifted a skinny old arm from beneath the covers and prepared an injection. "I had to wait for Mr. Hayden.

He wanted to come with me and visit with some of my patients."

"He's a doctor?" asked the old woman.

"No, he writes for a newspaper."

"Oh, we been hearing about him," said Grandma, and there was an edge of interest in her thin, fretful old voice. "What's he coming here for? We ain't nobody for him to write about."

As she gave the injection, Juliet glanced for a moment at Steve, who was standing near the foot of the bed.

"I tried to tell him that," Juliet told the old woman sweetly. "But he wouldn't believe me!"

"Stubborn, is he? Ain't all men?" Grandma's voice was stronger now, edged with scorn as she peered half-blindly at Steve. "Never seen one in my life that wasn't stubborn as a mule and contrary as all get-out. What you hoping to find out up here, young feller?"

"Why people insist on living up here instead of down in the valley where it's much warmer," Steve answered her lightly. "Your daughter's been telling me her husband works over at the county seat and only gets home for weekends."

"She ain't my daughter. Her man's my son." The old woman's voice was edged with the querulousness of age and weakness. "Sure he works at a job at the county seat. Ain't no jobs a feller can get in these parts. And with a mess o' young-'uns to feed, he's got to have a job, ain't he?"

"Well, of course," said Steve placatingly. "Too bad there aren't jobs in and around Haleyville for the men-folks, isn't it?"

"It sure is," the old woman agreed. "Reckon they ain't never going to be any jobs in these parts. Folks pack up and get away soon's they're old enough. My Ben, he stuck here trying to farm and raise hogs and chickens. But there wasn't no way to get 'em to market, so he had to leave."

"We'll have to be running along now, Grandma," said Juliet briskly. "I'll see you next Tuesday, or earlier if you need me."

"I'm thanking you," said Grandma

with the formal dignity of a *grande dame.*

As Steve and Juliet reached the front door, Mamie brought an old change purse out of her apron pocket, carefully fished out a quarter and extended it to Juliet, who accepted it gravely and dropped it into her bag.

Going down to the jeep, Steve looked down at Juliet, scowling.

"A whole quarter for driving out here and giving the old gal a shot of something to keep her going for another week?" he demanded.

Juliet eyed him coolly.

"Those who can pay what they can," she told him. "If they can't pay anything at all, they get the same service."

"But who pays for the medicine and supplies you use?"

"The county provides part. What they don't provide, Dr. Laura and I provide out of our own pockets," she told him.

"Then you and Dr. Laura are the people I should be writing about," he burst out.

Juliet turned on him fiercely as they reached the jeep, her eyes flashing green fire.

"Don't you dare!" she cried.

Steve threw up a hand and took a backward step as though to defend himself from an attack, and there was an infuriating twinkle in his eyes.

"O.K., O.K., lady, call off your dogs! I couldn't without your consent, of course."

"And that you'll never get!" she flashed.

The jeep was traveling on now, and for a moment he was silent, deep in thought. Then suddenly he said, "I don't know about that. Your consent, of course, I can't hope to get. But Dr. Laura's different. If she were convinced that it might increase the county's appropriation for the clinic, I'm not a bit sure she wouldn't consent."

Bitterness twisted Juliet's mouth as she recalled the scene with her mother that morning.

"Yes," she said grimly. "Mother and Grady seem convinced that you are going to be the salvation of Haleyville."

"And obviously you don't agree?" Steve asked curiously.

Tilting her chin defiantly and looking straight ahead, Juliet snapped, "I don't agree that Haleyville needs saving."

Steve sighed and muttered barely above his breath, "Boy, you really are a stubborn little critter, aren't you?"

But Juliet made no answer as she stopped the jeep, got out, lifted her bag and stalked up the steep slope to another cabin that might have been the twin of the one they had just left.

Here the patient was an old man, paralyzed, wrapped in blankets in a big chair beside the blazing fire. His companion was a woman who might have been in her eighties, and who scurried about, welcoming Steve and Juliet.

While she ministered to the old man the life-giving injection that would keep him going for another week, Juliet heard the murmur of Steve's and the old woman's voices at the back of the room, and set her teeth hard as she did what little she could for the old man.

When they left the house, the old woman said haltingly, "Miss Juliet, we didn't get no money from the young-'uns this week, so I reckon you'll just have to charge for what you done for Paw."

Juliet said quickly, "Now don't you worry a bit, Mrs. Hulsey. You know Dr. Laura and I are always glad to do anything we can for either of you."

"I reckon the young-'uns are having it a mite rough down to the city, Miss Julie, or they'd never forget us," the old woman said unhappily. "They're mighty good to Paw and me when they can be."

"Of course they are, Mrs. Hulsey. They're fine young people," Juliet tried to dissipate the old woman's embarrassment.

"We'll pay you just as soon as we can," the old woman insisted.

"Of course. Don't you worry about it," Juliet told her. "Do you need anything from the store? I'll be glad to bring it out."

The old woman lifted her head with pathetic pride.

"Oh, no, ma'am, Miss Julie. Paw and me, we've got all the vittles we need. There's plenty in the smokehouse, and the young-'uns fixed us up with a lot of canned foods and flour and coffee and such when they was here at Christmas.

"Well, if you need anything, Mrs. Hulsey, you get somebody to let me know," Juliet said gently.

"I sure will, Miss Julie. Somebody can bring you word," the old woman told her gratefully.

Steve was deeply thoughtful as they went out.

"That's an amazing old lady," he said as she started the jeep. "She told me that she and her husband had been married for seventy years. That seems incredible."

"Why? She was fourteen when they married and he was seventeen," Juliet pointed out curtly.

"I just meant that it seems incredible two people could live together that long."

"Yes," said Juliet. "They are very lucky."

"Lucky?" he repeated as though the word sounded very odd under the circumstances. "To have spent seventy years in that shack?"

Juliet shot him a hostile glance.

"It wasn't a 'shack' seventy years ago, and it really isn't now," she protested. "It's a snug, tight cabin that was built by their neighbors on land given to Paw Hulsey when he was sixteen by his father. It was the custom back then, when a boy married, for his father to give him acreage, all he could spare from the home farm, a cow, a mule and a clutch of chickens. Then the neighbors came and 'raised' the cabin."

"So Mrs. Hulsey was telling me. It's going to make a great column."

"I suppose you got a picture of her?" drawled Juliet.

He looked at her in surprise.

"Well, of course. It wouldn't be much of a column without a picture," he reminded her. "It will probably make the Sunday edition."

"Congratulations!" she mocked him bitterly.

"Thanks." He was quite undisturbed by her sarcasm. "The thing that is going to make this a real story is that they are seventy years married. You don't hear much about such marriages nowadays."

"Not in the 'fiat-lands,' I suppose," Juliet answered. "But up here people take the marriage ceremony very seriously; especially that bit about 'until death do us part'. Up here they really mean it. A divorce is unheard of here."

Steve leaned back and nodded, his eyes on the road ahead.

"It's really quite a place," he mused aloud, and Juliet did not bother to answer him.

The jeep came to a halt with its nose against a steep bank that marked the end of the road.

Steve looked about him as Juliet slid out of the jeep and reached into the back for her bag.

"Somebody lives here?" he demanded. "A hermit?"

"A lady who likes her privacy," Juliet informed him.

"Privacy?" Steve looked about at the sweep of mountains, the steep hill above the jeep, and shivered. "What the lady's got is isolation — a very large portion of it, I'd say."

"You needn't come along," Juliet told him. "I won't be long."

"Don't be silly," Steve answered, and followed her up the steep slope. "I'm very anxious to meet any woman who lives alone in an eagle's nest like this."

Juliet swung him a swift glance. But before she could express any reproof, she realized she had forgotten something and turned back to the jeep. She reached behind the seat and brought up a large plastic-wrapped package. Steve moved swiftly to relieve her of it even as she made a swift movement to stop him.

"A New York Sunday paper!" he marveled as he held up the large flat package and caught sight of the headlines shining through the smooth plastic. "Then this is the old girl who lives on a microscopic pension and spends a large part of it subscribing to a New York Sunday paper! Now I know I want to meet her. What in blazes do you suppose interests her in this?"

Juliet's eyes flashed.

"Do you read science fiction?" she asked, and he stared at her, puzzled.

"Well, sure."

"Then for the same reason you read science fiction, Miss Sarah likes to read the New York Sunday newspapers," she told him. "After all, the people in those newspapers must seem to her like creatures from another planet, and she marvels at their behavior. Does that seem so odd to you?"

"Well, not odd, exactly. But certainly not what I'd expect to find up here in a spot like this."

"And why not? Can't you imagine how she must spend hours of her long days and nights poring over those pictures and the accounts of the fabulous activities that go on in a city like that? Haven't you that much imagination?"

"Well, sure, I have a lot of imagination," Steve defended himself. "But I still find it downright peculiar that a woman with such a small income would deprive herself of things she really needs in order to get these papers."

"Well, that's strictly her business; not yours or mine," Juliet reminded him as she turned and started back up the slope toward the small cabin tucked beneath its overhanging shelf of rock and trees.

"Just the same — "

"Just the same," Juliet turned on him fiercely as they reached the steps leading to the narrow front porch, "you are not to ask her any questions or attempt to interview her. Miss Sarah is entitled to her privacy, and you are not going to invade it. I'd much rather you stayed out here on the porch while I see her."

Steve's grin was faint, little more than a grimace, and there was a determined look in his eyes.

"I just bet you would," he said. "But

there's not a chance, Pretty Thing; not a chance. A good newspaperman goes where he knows there is a story. And I sure smell one here."

Juliet caught her breath with a gasp of fury that thickened her voice as she cried out, "If you dare, I'll see that she sues you for invasion of privacy, if not for libel, slander and anything else Grady can think of."

Behind them the door had opened, and Miss Sarah stood there, an old shawl huddled about her thin shoulders, her eyes bright behind her spectacles, her crumpled old face touched with a warm, welcoming smile that faded as she saw Steve.

"Why, Julie dear," her voice was faintly uneasy, "I heard the jeep, but I didn't know you were bringing company with you."

"I didn't, either, until I was ready to leave home this morning," Juliet told her. "This is Steve Hayden, Miss Smithwick. He's a newspaper man, and he's up here doing stories about some of the local people. So be very careful what you say to him, or he'll put your picture in the paper."

Miss Sarah gasped and stepped back in such obvious alarm that Steve's brows furrowed in a faint, puzzled scowl. He spoke swiftly, "Not unless you want it there, Miss Smithwick."

"I don't, oh, I don't!" she cried out sharply, made an effort to control her sudden alarm and managed a faint attempt at a smile. "I mean, with all the pretty young girls around, why would you want a picture of a battered old creature like me? But come in, come in. It's still a bit airish out, and I've got a nice fire going."

Juliet and Steve followed her into the house, and she closed the door.

Steve was watching her closely as she received the bundle of newspapers Juliet held out to her and did not miss the tenderness with which she cradled them as she led the way into the cabin's main room.

It was neat, immaculate and cozy;

furnished with the handmade furniture Steve had become accustomed to seeing in all the cabins he had visited. There was a big old-fashioned bed in one corner, and it was neatly covered by a handmade quilt that even Steve's masculine eyes knew to be a collector's item.

While Juliet gave Miss Sarah her injection, Steve prowled unobstrusively about the room, hands sunk deep in his pockets, pausing now and then to glance through the small, deep set windows with their immaculate curtains looped back as though to bring the glorious view into the cabin.

Juliet and Miss Sarah were talking softly, and Steve turned from the window, his leg brushing against a table beside it. The table, rickety from age, tilted, and a huge scrapbook fell from it to the floor, spilling its content with a thud. Steve stooped and picked up the scrapbook. It fell open in his hands, and the picture of a very handsome young man, balancing himself aboard the deck of a sailing sloop, his cap cocked back on his head, a self-satisfied grin on his handsome face, looked up at him. Beneath the picture the caption read: "Gerard Davison, better known as Gerry, aboard his new racing sloop, the Sea Queen, in which he will race to Hawaii later in the season."

Miss Sarah glanced at him and cried out as she saw him looking at the scrapbook. She leaped to her feet with an agility startling in one of her years and sprang toward him, her eyes blazing as she grabbed the book from his hands and held it close to her.

"You stop prying, mister. You stop it this minute. You've got no right. This is my house, and this is my book, and I'd thank you to get out of my house and leave my things alone. Get out! Get out! Do you hear me?"

Juliet said harshly, "I think you'd better, Steve. Wait for me in the jeep. You've done enough damage here."

"I don't know what all the fuss is about," Steve complained. "I brushed against the table accidentally, the book spilled from it, and I simply picked it up to put it back where it belonged. Is that a crime?"

"It sure is, when you're in a body's house and you go snooping into private matters." Miss Sarah blazed at him with a force and a fury of which he would not have thought her capable. "You get out of here. And don't you never come back. You hear me?"

"I'll see that he doesn't, Miss Sarah," Juliet soothed the old woman. As she looked at Steve, her green eyes were blazing. "Go on, Steve. I have to get Miss Sarah quieted down before I can leave her. And it is all your fault, as you very well know, don't you?"

"I just picked up the blasted book," Steve exploded in anger.

"Well, just pick up your two feet, mister, and get yourself out of here, and fast." Miss Sarah's voice was shaking, and tears were slipping down her cheeks.

"I'm sorry," said Steve, and walked out of the house.

At the jeep, he stood for a long moment, hands jammed deep into his pockets, his brow furrowed thoughtfully, as he looked with unseeing eyes at the magnificent sweep of mountains before him. And then, very thoughtfully, he drew an envelope from his pocket and wrote down the name of the young man whose picture had looked up at him from the scrapbook in the ancient cabin.

Of course, he told himself, it could merely have been that Miss Sarah had cut the picture out and pasted it in the scrapbook because the young man was spectacularly good-looking. But somehow, Steve's instinct told him there was another explanation for the presence of the picture in this old cabin. And he would be a very poor newspaperman if he failed to discover what it was.

Juliet was cold-eyed, thin-lipped and very curt when she came down the steep slope to the jeep. She put her instrument case in the back of the jeep, slid behind the wheel and, as she switched on the ignition, gave Steve a hostile look.

"That's the first bad attack Miss Sarah has had in months, so you should be very proud of yourself," she told him.

"I am not proud of myself, but I don't feel guilty," Steve defended himself. "The book fell on the floor. What was I supposed to do — just let it lie there?"

"You didn't have to open it and start reading it!"

"I didn't open it. It fell open when I picked it up. It was quite apparent that it had been open at that spot so often that it just fell open automatically when it was picked up."

"Well, I promised her you wouldn't be out here again," Juliet said sharply.

Steve relaxed slightly and managed an unamused grin.

"That was a pretty safe promise," he assured her coolly, "since I'm going back to Atlanta this afternoon."

Juliet turned swiftly.

"You are? Oh, that's wonderful!" She beamed at him.

"Don't be so indecently glad to be rid of me," he protested, only half in jest. "It's an easy drive back up here.

And make no mistake about it. I will be back from time to time."

Juliet's beam vanished, and she said crossly, "I might have known it was too good to be true."

"I know I'll hate myself for asking this, but what was too good to be true?" Steve asked cautiously.

"That Haleyville was going to be rid of you permanently!" flung the words at him as if hoping they would bruise and burn.

Steve's grin told her how far short of the mark the words were.

"Oh, there are few really permanent things in this cockeyed, mixed up world of ours, Julie, my girl," he assured her in a casual tone that added quite unnecessary fuel to her fury. "And my staying away from Haleyville is not one of them! I'll be back. You can count on that. And you might even be glad to see me."

"That'll be the day!" Juliet told him hotly.

Steve studied her for a moment, and

the laughing twinkle went out of his eyes. He nodded as though at some secret thought that was very pleasant.

"Yes, Julie," he said gently. "That'll be the day. And *what* a day it's going to be!"

Juliet's hands clenched on the wheel, and her foot pressed hard on the accelerator, so that the jeep shot ahead much too fast toward the next curve.

6

SPRING came reluctantly to Haleyville, long after it had washed over the valleys, leaving drifts of crab apple and dogwood bloom and clusters of wild azaleas climbing the steep slopes up from the creek.

Making her morning rounds, Juliet saw winter quilts and blankets airing on clotheslines in back of cabins. Here and there red flannel underwear waved valiantly in the breeze, as though to boast that some mountain man had been brave enough to discard his winter heavies in favor of something less scratchy.

To Juliet it was a gloriously peaceful time. And she refused to admit even to herself that one of the joys of the burgeoning spring was the fact that Steve Hayden was no longer there.

One afternoon in the post office she encountered Miss Letitia Wentworth, the unpaid schoolteacher who had chosen to spend her retirement in Haleyville, doing a labor of love, teaching the mountain children not yet ready for the long trip to the Consolidated High School at the county line.

Miss Letty's plump, weathered face was beaming as she saw Juliet, and she held up a thick sheaf of mail.

"Just look, Julie, what the story that nice young man wrote about me has done," she said happily. "I've been hearing from old friends I'd lost track of years ago. And some people in Atlanta have sent shipments of books that are badly needed here and even checks to provide whatever we may need for our adult classes. Isn't it wonderful what a little newspaper publicity can do for a really worth-while enterprise? And don't tell me our elementary school isn't a worthwhile enterprise! You should see some of my adult pupils! I've never been busier or happier in my whole life."

"I'm so glad, Miss Letty," Juliet answered, and added, "You let Steve

Hayden write about you?"

Miss Letty looked astonished at the question.

"Well, for heaven's sake, why not?" she protested. "I'd have been grievously insulted if he hadn't wanted to! Didn't you see the story? It had my picture and a picture of the school. Why, Julie, it may even result in our getting a new school, the one we so desperately need. And there is going to be an improved road. Oh, it won't be paved, of course, at least not this year. But it will be in another year or two. It's being graded and filled in and widened. People can get in to Haleyville now, or they soon will be able to. And what's even more important, people who want to can get out of Haleyville and over to the hospital and to the county seat to shop. Why, we can even have summer visitors now that they will have a road and now that that nice Mr. Hayden has told them what a lovely place Haleyville is."

"What a lovely place it was." Juliet could not keep back the acid words.

Miss Letty stared at her, puzzled and resentful.

"Julie dear, what are you talking about?" she protested.

Juliet made a little gesture that tried to dismiss the question.

"I guess it's just that I love Haleyville the way it is, and I don't want it spoiled," she confessed. But even as she said it, she felt uncomfortably ashamed.

"Why, Julie, that's very selfish of you. And selfish is the very last thing I ever felt you could be accused of," Miss Letty scolded her. "Haleyville is a lovely quiet place, that's quite true. But quietness often means a town is dying. When the young people leave the place as soon as they are old enough to find jobs, because there are no jobs here, a town can't hope to go on growing. And Haleyville is much too historic and too cherished a place to be allowed to die!"

"I know, Miss Letty. It's just that I hate big cities," Julie admitted.

Miss Letty laughed, dropped a friendly

arm about her shoulder and gave her a little hug.

"Julie, don't be absurd." She laughed. "There's not the slightest danger of Haleyville ever growing into a big city, and I'm sure none of us want it to. But the people need jobs; not only the young people who can go away, but the older people with families. Take the Jed Lowery family, for instance. Jed has seven children and a wife; and he has a few acres of apple trees and a practically perpendicular farm. Now how could you expect Jed to make a living for his family here? He has to go over to the sawmill and work six days a week so the family can be fed. And he's only one of several other men in the same position."

"And just how would you arrange for Jed and the others to have jobs here?" Juliet demanded.

"Why, by luring some small industry to town, and building cottages and motels for the summer visitors we hope to have," Miss Letty pointed out as though surprised that this had not occurred to Juliet. "And then we have women who make lovely handmade quilts and chenille spreads and bath mats. There are small mountain communities all over the Blue Ridge Mountains that have banded together and gotten firms to come in and handle their products. There are so many, many things that could be done, Julie, if we all worked together on them. Why, the fishing and hunting alone would bring in visitors from all over the South. Once we let them know what we have to offer, you'll see. And that nice Mr. Hayden is working very hard to do just that."

She laughed and added, not entirely in jest, "Matter of fact, I think we should elect him mayor, or at least head of the Chamber of Commerce."

"If we had a Chamber of Commerce," Juliet mocked her.

Miss Letty's look of bright surprise appalled her.

"Why, haven't you heard? We do have a Chamber of Commerce, she gloated. "I admit it's only about twenty-four hours old, but we are organized and we're working. Your friend, Grady, is currently the head of it, but he insists it's only a temporary appointment until we get things going. However, I'm hoping we can persuade him to keep the job, at least until he's ready to enter politics. That's a very knowledgeable young man, Julie. You should be very proud of him."

"Oh, I am," Juliet answered.

"And you're a very lucky girl, Julie, to have him for your own," Miss Letty insisted.

"Very lucky indeed," Juliet answered, but there was a note in her voice that made Miss Letty eye her suspiciously.

"You haven't been quarreling with him, have you, Julie?" she demanded.

"Goodness, no! Why should I quarrel with him?"

"No reason at all that I can see," Miss Letty replied. "But then of course I'm not very knowledgeable about the ways of people in love, much to my regret!"

"Oh, I'm sure you don't really mean that, Miss Letty," Juliet said. "After all, nobody could have had a richer, fuller life than you have and are still having."

Miss Letty's mouth twisted slightly.

"Teaching other people's children? That makes for a full, rich life, Julie?" she asked wryly. "Don't you ever believe it, Julie. A teaching career can be and is very rewarding. But it's nothing like having children of your own. A home and a husband and children are a woman's trinity. And don't you ever doubt it. That's what I want for you, Julie, one of these days; for you and Grady."

"Well, thanks, Miss Letty. That's very sweet of you."

Juliet spoke awkwardly, and Miss Letty's eyes narrowed slightly.

"You haven't done anything foolish, have you, Julie?" she demanded.

Puzzled and a bit apprehensive, Juliet asked, "Such as what, Miss Letty?"

"Oh, such as taking a second look at some dashing stranger like Steve Hayden, for instance, and maybe thinking you were in love with him?"

Juliet gasped as though the words had

been a slap in the face, and her eyes blazed with green fire.

"Miss Letty, what an outrageous thing to say! I loathe Steve Hayden!" she burst out.

Miss Letty grinned wryly.

"That's too bad, Julie," she said gently.

"That I hate and despise the man?" Miss Letty nodded slowly. "Because both love and hate are violent emotions and the dividing line between the two is very thin. Sometimes you step over it from hate to love without even realizing it."

Juliet set her teeth hard against the angry words that threatened to spill out. And as though she sensed the turmoil in Juliet's mind, Miss Letty put out her hand and touched Juliet's. Miss Letty's eyes were kind and warm and friendly.

"Pay no attention to me, Julie dear," she said gently. "I'm a meddlesome, interfering, snooping old maid, and I'm always sticking my nose into other people's business. It's only because I'm genuinely fond of you and of Grady that I spoke out. Forget it, and forgive me?"

Juliet said through her teeth, entirely without warmth, "Of course, Miss Letty. I know you were only fooling."

Miss Letty's eyes held a faint and entirely unexpected twinkle.

"Do you now?" Her tone was faintly mocking. "Well, I'll have to be running along. I have to get material ready for my adult class this evening. I'll see you again soon, I hope, Julie."

"I hope so, too, Miss Letty," Juliet said politely but without undue warmth.

As she drove back to the clinic, parked the jeep and went into the house, Juliet was still seething with the anger Miss Letty's words had aroused within her. In love with Steve Hayden! She'd never heard a more preposterous accusation.

But it was only a few weeks later, as she came back from her rounds to the clinic, that she saw Steve's car ahead of her in the drive, and her crazy heart flipped.

She sat very still for a long moment behind the wheel of the jeep before she pulled herself together and got out.

Carrying her well-worn black medical kit, she walked across the drive, spoke to two or three patients who were waiting to be treated by Dr. Laura as soon as office hours began, and went into the house.

Dr. Laura had been watching for her and came to meet her, drawing her into the small private office beyond the examination room. There Steve waited for her; Steve and a tall, handsome young man with a worried expression who looked as if he'd been through quite an ordeal and knew more was coming.

"Hello, Julie," said Steve quietly. "You're looking wonderful. But then, you always do."

Julie said, "Thanks," and glanced questioningly at the stranger, who was watching her with a curiously intent gaze.

"Julie, this is Gerard Davison," said Steve, and Juliet nodded politely. "Gerry, this is Juliet Cochran, who takes care of the patients who can't get in to the clinic."

"Then I owe you a very great deal,

Miss Cochran," said Gerard, and his pleasantly baritone voice had a faint touch of huskiness.

Puzzled, Juliet looked from one man to the other and said, bewildered, "I don't understand."

"Thank you for taking what Steve tells me is superb and devoted care of — my mother," said Gerard.

Juliet stared at him and then at Steve. And Steve said words that fell like a bomb in that small room: "Gerard is the son of your Miss Sarah Smithwick."

For a stunned moment Juliet could only stare at him, quite sure he had lost his mind, and then she said sharply, "I don't believe it!"

Gerard grinned ruefully, but it was a grin quite without mirth.

"I don't blame you, Miss Cochran," he confessed. "I didn't, either, until Steve brought incontrovertible proof. There's no possibility of a mistake. I'm quite convinced of that. And I'd like to see my mother."

Juliet was glad to find a chair behind

her. She dropped into it, because her shaking knees were threatening to give way beneath her. She stared at Steve, her green eyes dazed, bewildered.

"Why, this is the most fantastic thing I ever heard in my life," she exploded at last, her voice shaking. "This is some crazy idea of yours."

"It isn't, Julie. It's the sober truth. There can be no possible doubt about it," Steve assured her with convincing sincerity.

Juliet looked at Gerard, who was watching her anxiously. He was spectacularly good-looking, in his late twenties, well-tailored, well-groomed, the very picture of a wealthy young man, as out of place in the little town as a peacock would have been in a mountain barn yard.

Gerard said after a moment, "I can imagine how you must feel, Miss Cochran. But I wonder if you can imagine how I felt when Steve brought me this fantastic story."

"I'm afraid I can't," Juliet replied faintly.

"You see," Gerard seemed anxious for her to understand and quite willing to explain, "I had always been told that my mother died when I was born. My father died twelve years ago. There was never any indication that I had any relatives except a couple of uncles and a few cousins. So when Steve came along with this story, I suppose I was pretty anxious to believe him. But even if I hadn't been, the proof he brought me would have convinced even the most unwilling Doubting Thomas."

Juliet made a little helpless gesture with a hand that shook slightly.

"But Miss Sarah!" she protested. "Surely it couldn't have been Miss Sarah!"

"It was Mrs. Gerard Davison Senior, who bore him, Julie," Steve told her gently. "Davison Senior was down here with a group of men on a hunting trip. Miss Sarah was an exquisitely beautiful young girl, and Davison persuaded her to elope with him, since her father was one of the guides for the hunting party and had forbidden any of the party to so much as speak to Sarah. When she eloped with Davison and they were married in another state, the Smithwicks refused to have anything more to do with her. They just pretended she had gone off to a job and let it go at that."

"The Smithwicks were always people who liked to keep to themselves, Julie, remember?" Dr. Laura said.

"And then she came back here, leaving a son behind her? That doesn't sound like Miss Sarah at all," protested Juliet. "No matter how unhappy she had been — but then why should she have been unhappy?"

"I'm afraid that's something only Miss Sarah can tell us," said Steve, and stood up, his eyes grim. "Shall we go?"

Juliet looked up at him and at Gerard, who had also risen.

"Go where?" she demanded.

"Don't be silly!" Steve's voice held more than a hint of reproof. "Why, to see Miss Sarah, of course, and let her tell us why she came back here, leaving a baby son behind, and has never told anybody anything about those lost years when she lived in New York as the wife of a fabulously wealthy man."

Juliet lifted wide eyes to Gerard, who was watching her anxiously.

"Your father was a very wealthy man?" she asked.

"I'm afraid so, Miss Cochran."

"And that means you are, too?"

"And you're wondering how I'd let my mother live in dire poverty — "

"I'm not wondering any such thing, because she has been happy — "

"And that's the reason she subscribed to a New York Sunday newspaper and kept a scrapbook of all his pictures?" That was Steve's voice, coolly deliberate.

Julie turned on him furiously.

"You had no right to do this to her!" she flared.

"Please don't feel that way, Miss Cochran," Gerard insisted. "He's done me a service for which I can never thank him enough."

"But what has he done to Miss Sarah — tearing her whole life up by the roots, bringing out into the open something that she has kept jealously secret for all these years?" cried Juliet.

"Now, Julie, if she's been saving his pictures all these years, denying herself things so that she can have the newspapers, don't you suppose she'll be glad to see him, to know that he cared enough about her to make an effort to find her?" Dr. Laura asked.

Gerard looked painfully abashed.

"That's kind of you, Dr. Cochran," he told her. "But I'm afraid I'm not entitled to such kindness. You see, I thought she was dead; it never occurred to me to question that. It's Steve who has gone to the trouble of proving to me that I do have a mother and that she is alive, and now I'm going to see her. That's something for which I can never thank Steve enough."

Juliet said viciously, "Oh, don't thank him. He was just doing his job, getting a story for that paper of his."

Steve studied her coolly for a long moment before he nodded and said quietly, "That's right. And it'll be a really great story, too."

Juliet glared at him incredulously.

"You mean you *are* going to write the story?" she gasped.

Steve seemed surprised at the question; even a little resentful that she should ask it.

"Well, of course. Why not, since Gerard has given me permission?"

"Oh, so *he's* given you permission! How about Miss Sarah? Or aren't you going to bother even asking her?" Juliet demanded.

"Of course. That's why we are going out there now to see her," Steve answered.

"Will you come with us, Miss Cochran?" asked Gerard anxiously.

Juliet looked from one to the other and drew a deep breath.

"I will, of course, because somebody's going to have to be there to cushion the shock for her. You'd better not come out until tomorrow."

"We're going now," Steve cut in.

Juliet glared at him, outraged.

"You can't just barge in on her like this, without a word of warning, without preparing her for such a shock. Her heart — "

"Dr. Laura says her heart is in excellent condition and that there is no danger of a shock," Steve insisted.

Gerard said quietly, "I've waited twenty-six years to see her, Miss Cochran. Don't make me wait any longer, please."

Juliet stared at him, bemused, bewildered, so completely rocked by the whole fantastic business that she scarcely realized what she was saying.

"You've waited twenty-six years, but you can't wait twenty-four hours longer, even if you know it will be better for her?" she managed at last.

Gerard's smile was very faint and entirely without mirth.

"But you're forgetting that in those twenty-six years I didn't even know she existed. Now that I do — well, surely you must understand, Miss Cochran, that I must see her."

"Let's go," said Steve, and held out

his hand to Juliet. But she struck it down furiously and turned and stalked toward the door and out to the jeep.

Gerard looked uncertainly at the jeep and then back at Steve's car.

"Shouldn't we follow? There's scarcely room in the jeep for all three of us, is there?"

"The jeep is the only thing on wheels that can travel the road to the Smithwick place," Steve told him. He motioned him into the jeep beside Juliet and crowded in beside him.

Juliet's jaw was set as she drove, her hands clenched tightly on the wheel. And neither of the men spoke as the jeep made its way along the narrow, twisting, makeshift road.

Gerard looked about him at the truly awe-inspiring scenery. When at last the jeep stopped, he looked up at the small cabin perched on top of the hill, with the overhanging cliff seeming to offer it protection.

"My mother lives here?" he asked as though he could not believe it.

"Except for the two or three years she spent as Mrs. Gerard Davison, she has lived here all her life and wouldn't want to live anywhere else," Juliet told him curtly, and led the way up the path.

The door of the cabin opened as they reached the steps, and Miss Sarah stood there, her sleeves rolled above her wrists, an apron tied about her middle, a cooking spoon in one hand.

"Why Julie dear, you're back. Did you forget something?" she asked before she saw the two men.

For a stunned moment she looked at Steve and bristled. Then her eyes found Gerard, and all the blood left her face and her eyes became wild and terrified. The hand holding the cooking spoon relaxed, and it clattered to the floor as she clung to the door frame for support, her body shaken.

There was a long, stunned moment that seemed to Juliet and Steve to stretch endlessly before Miss Sarah whispered, "Gerard!"

Gerard's shocked eyes had taken in

the scrupulously neat but shabby cabin; and the woman before him in a calico dress beneath an apron, her hair clasped back into a bun at the back of her head. For the barest instant, Juliet thought she saw on his face a look of shock, even of revulsion; and then he put out his arms and gathered Miss Sarah's shaking body and held it close. She leaned against him, too feeble to draw herself free of his arms.

Steve looked down at Juliet with a triumphant look, which Juliet returned with one of deep hostility.

Miss Sarah said at last, her voice thick with sobs, "Oh, Gerard, you shouldn't have come. You shouldn't have tried to find me. It was so much better the way it was."

Gerard said gently, "It wasn't, Mother! It wasn't at all. After all the years when I thought I'd lost my mother, finding her again is about the most wonderful thing in the world. Why did you run off and leave me, Mother? Why didn't you bring me with you?"

Miss Sarah laughed shakily, and her work-roughened hand made a little gesture that took in the scene around them. She said unsteadily, "From your father's fancy home to this? Oh, no, Sonny, I couldn't do that to you. I couldn't stay there, like a fish out of water; but I knew you'd grow up in those surroundings, and you'd be all right."

She had managed to pull herself together somewhat, and now her ingrained, deeply rooted sense of hospitality took over as she ushered them into the house.

Gerard seated her in a big chair and drew a stool forward so he could sit near her. His eyes were taking her in hungrily, and Miss Sarah was stealing proud, shy glances at him as though she could not make herself believe that he was really here, where she had never dreamed that he would be.

"Well, now," she breathed at last, put both shaking hands to her face and pushed back a strand of hair that had escaped from its neat bun, "I suppose,

Julie, you and Mr. Hayden, and you, Sonny, are wondering how it all happened. I've kept it a secret for so long that I don't quite know where to begin."

Gerard smiled at her. "Steve found out that you eloped with Dad and went to New York to live, until I was born. Then you checked out on him — and on me — and came back here. Suppose you fill us in on why you ran out on us."

There was a tinge of color on Miss Sarah's weathered face and she made a little deprecating movement with one work-roughened hand.

"Well, now, I reckon maybe most of what happened was my fault," she told him earnestly. "You see, my Paw had been a hunting and fishing guide most of my life. He was awful strict with me. Didn't want me to meet up with any of the men he guided. But somehow your Paw and me met anyway. And it was like suddenly a woods fire had broke out. We knew right from the start how it was going to be with us."

She broke off shyly, and her smile was abashed.

"I reckon it's hard for you to believe it, Sonny, but I was a right pretty girl in those days." She seemed to be apologizing. "I was just past my eighteenth birthday, and your Paw was twice my age. But he hadn't ever married, and he told me it was because he had never met a girl before that he wanted to marry. He wanted to marry me and I wanted to marry him, so we just took things into our own hands and eloped, because we both knew Paw would never consent to us getting married."

"You're low-grading yourself when you say you were 'a right pretty girl,'" Gerard protested warmly. "You are exquisitely beautiful; the big portrait of you in the drawing room proves that."

Miss Sarah's eyes widened.

"My sakes alive!" she breathed in awe. "You mean you still got that old picture?"

"Still got it? Why, it's my proudest possession — a portrait of my mother painted by a world-famous artist in the first few months of her marriage to my father! In case of a fire in the place, all the servants have been warned that even if nothing else can be saved, that must be rescued."

She beamed at him, and Juliet, a silent but intently interested witness, thought in amazement, Why, she's not old at all! I thought she was. But she looks — why, right this minute, she looks as young as springtime.

"Well, now I'm right glad to know that," said Miss Sarah, her whole attention centered on Gerard, as though Steve and Juliet were not even in the cabin. "I always thought it was a right pretty picture, but I thought maybe after I left it might get put away somewhere out of sight."

"Well, it hasn't been and isn't going to be, ever," Gerard assured her firmly. "But go on. You haven't told us yet why you ran out on Dad and me."

"It was for your own sakes, Sonny," she told him with a rather pathetic honesty.

"I was making your Paw — your Dad — perfectly miserable, and there wasn't anything I could do about it but get out of your lives."

"But why?" he persisted.

"Because I just didn't fit in with your Dad's friends," she answered. "How could I? I was just a backwoods country girl who'd never been farther away from this cabin than the county seat, and then not more than three or four times in my life."

"But if you and Dad loved each other — "

"We did, oh, we did!" There was a touching ring of sadness and bitter sincerity in Miss Sarah's voice. "But I saw that I was just shaming him and making him embarrassed in front of his fancy friends. And the servants frightened me. They despised me, and I knew it."

"Why didn't you tell Dad and have him fire the whole lot of them? It's what I'd have done," Gerard told her warmly.

Miss Sarah smiled at him.

"It would have been the same with any new servants he might have hired and it wouldn't have helped a bit," she insisted.

She drew a deep breath and went on.

"Well, I suppose I may as well tell you the rest of it. We went across the state line and were married. And then we stopped in Charleston, and your father bought me a lot of beautiful clothes; more clothes, I felt, then I'd live long enough to wear. But he didn't seem to think much of them, for all that I thought they were so beautiful. He just said they would have to do until we got back to New York, and then I could be 'properly fitted and have specially designed clothes'."

She was silent for a moment, her thoughts turned back, until at last she resumed, her voice soft with the memories of that long ago day.

"Well, when we got to New York, I discovered that 'home' was a big, fine apartment right up on top of a building so tall that it seemed to me I ought to be able to stand out on the terrace and pick a basketful of stars any time I wanted to." She still marveled at the memory. "And the apartment was two stories high. I'd never seen an apartment before, and certainly not one that had stair-steps and a balcony running around and a terrace outside big long windows."

Gerard's hand touched hers gently, and she again gave him that sweet, shy smile that brought the sting of tears to Juliet's eyes.

"Well, when we got off the elevator, there was a lot of people all lined up to welcome us," she went on slowly. "And me, being the fool girl I was, decided they were friends of his that had come to welcome us and thought how neighborly it was of them. And then I found out they were all servants. There was a stiff man in a funny-looking coat and striped vest and black pants that your father said was the butler; and a very sour-looking woman he said was the housekeeper; and there were maids and a cook and a cook's helper — oh, such a crowd of people that were all servants just to wait on two people. And I guess right there was where it all started."

Gerard said quietly, "Where it all started?"

Miss Sarah nodded, "Your father realized he'd made an awful mistake when he married me."

"But you were both in love," Gerard said gently.

"Oh, yes, we were both in love, and we tried very hard to make it work," she answered slowly. "I tried very hard to be what I knew he wanted me to be, to be able to feel at home with his friends. And there was so many of them. The women were all so beautifully dressed and so sure of themselves. And the men were — well, I think I must have amused them by the things I said and did, not knowing any better. But most of all, I think it was the servants that really convinced me I had no rights there."

For the first time she seemed to become aware of Juliet and Steve and included them in what she was trying so hard to explain.

"You see, I'd always had a lot to do here at home," she explained. "I'd never just sat with my hands folded while other people waited on me. I wasn't used to having breakfast in bed; having a maid to draw my bath, to help me dress, to take care of my clothes. The first time I cleaned my own room the maid gave notice; and the housekeeper warned me it mustn't happen again. But I was only trying to use up some of the time that I had more of than I knew what to do with."

She looked down at Garard, and a faint smile touched her face.

"Your father thought it was pretty silly of me to want to keep busy, and said I should take some courses in how to live up to my new position. So I did. I learned about how to enter a room gracefully; and how to order a meal in a smart restaurant and how to be insolent to the servants. Only they despised me even more, I think, after I started being bossy and nasty than when I'd been scared to death of them. I guess maybe they knew I was still scared of them, and that's why they didn't pay any attention to me. I was rushing around from pillar to post, what with all these courses your father wanted me to take; and he had gotten so tired of me that I didn't see very much of him any more. Then we found out that you were coming."

A look of ineffable radiance touched her face, and her eyes were misty with tenderness as she dwelt lovingly on those memories.

"Your father was so happy at the thought that he was going to have a son," she went on after a moment. "For of course from the very first minute the doctor said I was pregnant, it was your father's conviction that the baby would be a son. It never seemed to occur to him that it could be anything else. And I was so happy that I forgot all about being afraid of the servants, and looked forward to the time when I'd have my own baby to take care of and to fill my days."

She was silent, and after a moment

Gerard said quietly, "And so?"

She looked at him and made an odd little gesture.

"And so when I came home from the hospital, the baby was taken out of my arms. And from that day on I was allowed to see him for maybe fifteen or twenty minutes a day, with a nurse standing ready to take him out of my arms the minute the time was up. Sometimes she'd let me watch her give him his bath; but she'd never let me touch him. My own baby son!"

An old grief that had lain in her heart for twenty-six years was expressed in those last words.

"But surely if you had told Dad — " Gerard began.

Miss Sarah smiled sadly, "Oh, he agreed with the nurse that I didn't know anything about taking care of a baby. She was a very fine, carefully trained nurse who specialized in taking care of babies. He said I was to do exactly as she said, and not to try to interfere. Sometimes at night when the nurse was asleep, I'd slip in and look at you. But she always slept with one eye open, as she said, and she always caught me and complained to your father, threatening to leave if I didn't stop 'disturbing' her and the baby. And of course your father always sided with her, because you were the most important thing in his life, and he was convinced the nurse knew more about the proper care of a baby than I did."

She drew a deep breath, and then she spread her hands in a hopeless gesture.

"So you see why I felt I was just in the way there, and there was nothing for me to do but come back home. Paw and Maw took me in, and we didn't tell anybody anything. Living out here like we did, we didn't have any neighbors to be too curious."

Her story was finished, and she seemed very wearied by the telling of it.

Gerard bent forward and touched her cheek with his lips, and her eyes flew wide with astonished delight. He stood up, holding one of her hands in both of his, and looked at Steve and Juliet.

"Would you mind leaving us alone for a little while? There are things we have to say to each other without an audience," he said stiffly.

"Sure thing," said Steve. He took Juliet's arm and urged her out of the cabin to the front steps.

He looked down at her flushed face and tear-filled eyes and said gently, "It's all right now, Julie. They've found each other."

Juliet turned on him furiously.

"And I suppose you're feeling very proud of yourself!" she flashed.

Steve stared at her, frowning in surprise at her anger.

"Well, as a matter of fact, I am," he told her sharply. "Look, if you think this was easy, my girl, you're entitled to another think! I worked for weeks digging all this up; and then it took me some more weeks to contact Davison and convince him that I knew what I was talking about, and to prove to a whole raft of lawyers that it was true. I got a whiff of an idea from seeing that scrapbook full of pictures of a Gerard Davison, practically from babyhood to his present age; it solved the mystery of why she was willing to make sacrifices to buy the New York newspapers. And from then on, it was a real challenge. I was determined to prove what I suspected, and I have. And now, as you say, I *do* feel proud of the job I did."

"It sounds exactly like something you would do." Juliet knew she was being unfair and illogical, but she couldn't keep back the words. "Miss Sarah was living here in quiet and peace. All of the past was behind her, buried with her memories. And you had to go dig it all up and bring that man here. So what's to happen now?"

Steve stared at her, puzzled and on the defensive.

"What do you mean?" he asked.

"Does he stay here with her? Or does he take her back to New York with him to subject her to more unhappiness? I suppose that's what he'll want to do.

Somehow, I can't picture him settling down here with her, any more than I can imagine Miss Sarah willing to go back to the life she tried to live with his father. So, I repeat, what happens now?"

Steve gave her a cold, unfriendly look.

"That's something for them to decide, don't you think?" he reminded her.

Juliet's brows went up airily, and she drawled with venomous sweetness, "Oh, are you going to let *them* decide?"

"And why not?"

"Oh, I had an idea you had it all planned out for them."

Steve dropped his hands on her shoulders and swung her about to face him. His eyes were blazing, and his jaw was set sternly.

"You are the most exasperating creature it has ever been my misfortune to encounter," he told her, his voice low and rough with anger. "For two cents I'd turn you across my knee and wallop the daylights out of you."

Juliet caught her breath, and her eyes

were wide. But before she could manage an answer, Steve finished furiously, "And don't tempt me by saying I wouldn't dare! I can't think of anything at the moment I'd rather do! It's way past time when somebody should have done it!"

He held her so for just a moment, a moment that seemed to Juliet to stretch endlessly. The fire in his eyes died out, and his hands on her shoulders relaxed slightly. There was an instant when she felt sure that he would draw her close in his arms and hold her tightly. But the next moment, before he could follow that impulse, his hands dropped away, and he turned and went plunging down the path toward the waiting jeep.

Juliet leaned against the porch post, her knees shaking, a wild crazy clamor in her heart to which she refused to listen. Yet she knew she could never escape its surging demand, however hard she tried to turn away from it.

7

THE publication of Steve's story in the Atlanta paper created a nine days' sensation in Haleyville and in many much larger cities, including New York.

There were a few days during which Haleyville's one hotel was hard put to it to take care of the photographers and newsmen that came from nearby cities, intent on getting the story of the little old woman who had suddenly been identified as the widow of one of the country's wealthiest men and mother of one of the country's most eligible young bachelors.

Juliet felt it was to Gerard's eternal credit that he moved into the hotel and established himself as the person to whom the newspaper people should go for information about his mother. He was very careful about taking anyone out to visit her and saw to it that she knew well in advance of such an invasion of her privacy. There were pictures, of course, which under the circumstances could not be avoided. But with Gerard there to protect her from unwarranted invasion, Miss Sarah seemed to bloom beneath the barrage of interviews and pictures.

When Juliet came to see her the week after the publicity began, Miss Sarah looked half the age Juliet had thought her. She was neatly, almost smartly dressed in a becoming dark frock, and her hair had been done by Haleyville's leading and only hairdresser. The cabin was as it had always been, though, and Juliet was grateful that Gerard had not tried to overwhelm his mother with new and expensive furnishings.

When Juliet had completed her examination, she laughed, replaced her supplies in her worn bag and snapped it shut.

"I was worried about you, Miss Sarah," she admitted frankly. "I was afraid that all this fuss and fury might have upset you and you might be needing me badly. But now that I see you're in the pink, there won't be any need for my services for you from now on."

"Oh, yes, there will, Julie dear," Miss Sarah protested anxiously. "Oh, maybe not for any medical treatment. I never felt so well in my life. But I'd miss you so, Julie, if you didn't come out every week. Yet I know I haven't any right to expect you to, as busy as you are."

"But you won't be staying here long, Miss Sarah. Won't you be going away when your son does?" asked Juliet.

A look of terror touched Miss Sarah's eyes.

"Oh, no, Julie, no! I'd never leave here! I couldn't go back to New York!"

Juliet said gently, "But, Miss Sarah, I'm sure Gerard would take very good care of you and not let the servants bully you."

"Oh, I'm sure he would, too," Miss Sarah answered. "But, Julie, he's a young man. He has a right to a life of his own.

He'll find a nice girl in his own world and marry her and raise a family. He wouldn't want me hanging on his coat-tails."

She added hastily, "Oh, he thinks now that he would. He insists that I go back with him, or that I let him buy me a nice little house, maybe in Florida or California, and hire a companion to live with me and look after me." Her expression gave an indication of just how very unattractive she found the idea. "Julie, please help me convince him that I should stay right here where I've lived all my life! I don't want to leave. I'm perfectly all right here."

"But, Miss Sarah, how can I help you convince him of that?" Juliet asked.

"Well, he thinks a lot of you, Julie. And he says he'll always be grateful to you and Dr. Laura for taking such good care of me all these years. He'll listen to you. I know he will. Julie, help me convince him."

There was such an agony of pleading in her voice that Juliet put an arm about her and gave her a comforting hug.

"Now, now, Miss Sarah, don't get all wrought up," she soothed the woman. "I'm sure if you convince him that you are happier here than you would be anywhere else, he'll be willing for you to stay."

"I hope so, Julie. Oh, how I hope so." Miss Sarah's voice was shaken as she looked about her at the familiar, shabby room. "This is home, Julie. I just couldn't tear off and go away somewhere that's strange to me, even with Sonny. I'm very proud of him and very glad we found each other. But I don't want to leave here. Why, Julie, if I woke up in the morning and looked out of the window and couldn't see those mountains, and if I didn't have things to do all day to keep me busy — why, Julie, I'd just purely go out of my mind."

She looked out of the windows and saw the mountains stretching away, fold on fold, each fold growing bluer and bluer in the distance; the sun glancing down in bright glory over trees and rocks and the steep valley.

"Julie," her voice now was almost a whisper, "just the thought of being waited on hand and foot, of having nothing to do all day long, and seeing only people I don't even know frightens me. I can't leave all this, Julie — my friends and neighbors; my chickens and the guineas and the little wild things I feed all winter and in summer, too. Julie. I can't give it all up and go somewhere strange. Oh, Julie, help me make him see that!"

"I'll try, Miss Sarah," Juliet promised.

"He's a good boy and I love him, and I'm grateful that he would want me with him," Miss Sarah added hastily as though afraid that she might seem ungrateful for all that Gerard wanted to do for her. "But he doesn't understand. I've spent all my life here, except for those few years in New York when I was so miserable."

Even now, after all the years that lay between, memories of that time had the power to make Miss Sarah shiver.

She looked down at the dress she wore, and her hands touched the smooth waves of her hair. She looked up at Juliet and said softly, in the tone of a conspirator, "Sonny thinks that I should be dressed up like this all the time, Julie, but he doesn't understand. I'd a sight rather wear my own clothes that I can wash and iron myself. And I like sitting here in the afternoon, piecing quilts and maybe reading the newspapers and doing the things I've always done. I just don't want to go away."

Juliet bent down and touched Miss Sarah's cheek with her lips and tasted the salt of tears on the cheek.

"Well, if you don't want to, then you're not going to have to, Miss Sarah," she said firmly. "We'll convince Gerard that you don't want to go away with him, and he will go off and leave you alone as you want to be."

"He says he worries about me up here all-soul-alone and thinks maybe something bad might happen to me and I might not be able to get help," Miss Sarah told her. "But, Julie, I'm not an old helpless woman! The forties isn't old, is it, for somebody that's always had good health and worked hard and taken care of herself?"

"Of course not, Miss Sarah. Why, that's just the prime of life." Juliet smiled at her warmly.

Miss Sarah said with frank relief, "Well, you're the one that can convince him of that, Julie. You know my health is good. I suppose the fact you come out here once a week to do for me makes him think I'm right sickly. But I'm not, and you know it, Julie. So you must make him believe it."

Juliet said reluctantly, "Well, of course you're in good health, Miss Sarah, and I come out to see you once a week for a purely social visit more than for a nursing call. I come to see you because you are a person of whom I am very fond, and you give me a lift after the calls I make on people who really need me badly. But after all, there is something in what Gerard says about your being alone here and perhaps having an accident and not being able to call for help."

Miss Sarah nodded.

"Well, yes, I guess maybe so," she agreed unhappily. "But, Julie, I am at home here. I wouldn't be anywhere else. I've read in the newspapers about those 'nursing homes' and 'homes for the aged,' and they sound so depressing! I know I wouldn't like them a single little bit."

Juliet laughed. "Well, you're not eligible for either of those sort of places, so don't worry about it. And I promise you I'll talk to Gerard, and do my level best to convince him that he should let you stay right where you are! And now I'll have to be running along. It's almost time for afternoon clinic hours, and Dr. Laura will need me. I'll see you again soon, Miss Sarah; maybe even before next week."

As she went down the steep path to where the jeep waited, she turned and looked back at the cabin. Miss Sarah was going out across the back yard with a pan of scraps for the two pigs grunting in their pen, and Juliet tried to picture Miss Sarah 'being waited on hand and foot' by supercilious servants. But the picture wouldn't come. Miss Sarah was a mountain woman, part of the mountains, and she could no more be transplanted to some other spot than could one of the ancient mountains pines that had stood there for so many years, bending to the fury of mountain storms but not breaking. Miss Sarah had withstood storms and had never given an inch. And somehow, Juliet knew as she headed back for the clinic, a way had to be found to convince Gerard of that. She knew it was going to be a very difficult task, but somehow she had to do it, because she had promised Miss Sarah. Moreover, she could understand to a surprising degree just how Miss Sarah felt about being uprooted. It was as she herself would feel, though perhaps to a lesser degree, since she had not had the years of privacy and isolation that Miss Sarah cherished so deeply.

She reached the clinic a little before office hours began. The usual patients were scattered about the lawn, beneath the trees, on the old benches, and smiled and greeted her as she arrived.

Inside, Mattie was serving lunch to Dr. Laura. As Juliet came in, Mattie turned from the stove and said briskly, "Well, it's right nice you got here in time to swallow a few mouthfuls 'fore you and your Maw have to get back to work."

"Make it more than a few mouthfuls, Mattie. I'm starved!" Juliet said as she took her place at the table.

Dr. Laura smiled at her warmly.

"How is Miss Sarah?" she asked.

"Scared to death," Juliet answered.

Dr. Laura's brows went up in surprise.

"Scared? Now why should she be scared?" she wondered. "She's not ill?"

"Not physically; just mentally. Seems her millionaire son wants to take her away from here to live with him in New York, and she's petrified at the prospect."

"But of course he wouldn't want to go away and leave her here, now that he has discovered her after all these years."

"There are times," said Juliet grimly

as she buttered a corn muffin, "when I could wish Steve Hayden had never come to Haleyville!"

"Don't tell me you're still hating poor Steve!"

"Poor Steve my eye!" There was a perceptible edge to Juliet's voice. "Things were going along peacefully until he came. Miss Sarah was happy and living the way she wanted to live. And then he had to come snooping and prying and blowing the lid off a secret she had kept hidden for more than twenty years! Yes, I still hate Steve Hayden, and I expect to go on hating him until I'm much older than Miss Sarah is at this moment."

Dr. Laura gave her a resigned smile.

"Well, I'm all fresh out of any arguments to persuade you to drop that attitude toward Steve," she admitted. "Personally, I like him a lot. And he was just doing his job. I'm sure Gerard Davison is deeply grateful to him."

"I suppose," Juliet agreed unwillingly. "Miss Sarah wants me to convince Gerard that he must go away and leave her here just as he found her, living the life she wants to live."

"Oh, but I'm sure he won't want to do that, Julie! He's too delighted to have found a mother he thought he had lost when he was only a baby! He wants to make up to her for the years that have been lost between them."

"But if that is only going to make her unhappy all over again," protested Julie, "would it be fair to her? Mother, don't you realize that only a depth of misery that we can't even hope to understand could have persuaded her to run away when she did?"

Dr. Laura flung up both hands in a little gesture of protest.

"Hey, now, wait a minute. I'm not the one you have to convince! Save your arguments for Gerard. He's going to stop by this afternoon when he gets back from the county seat. He wants to see you and to try to thank you for what you've done for Miss Sarah."

"Good! Then maybe I can convince him," Juliet answered. "I was wondering how I'd get in touch with him."

Dr. Laura looked amused.

"Well, I don't think you'll have any trouble about that. He's been right here in Haleyville, at the hotel, for weeks. I wonder how he stands it, after what he must have been accustomed to all his life."

"Just the sheer novelty, I imagine, don't you?" Juliet answered.

"Sounds likely," Dr. Laura assented, smiling.

It was late afternoon when Gerard presented himself at the clinic; the last patient had just been dismissed.

Juliet was in the examination room, tidying it after the last patient had departed, when he appeared in the doorway, tall, spectacularly handsome in the gray slacks and well-tailored sports coat, his dark head bare.

"Hello. Dr. Laura said I'd find you here," he greeted her. "How about coming outside for a walk? That is, if you aren't too tired?"

"I'm not tired at all, and I'd love to

watch the sunset from a favorite spot of mine," Juliet assured him as they walked out together, across the back lawn and to a narrow, winding path that led between the trees and down a moderately steep slope, to a huge rock that jutted out from the side of the mountain.

Below them, the mountains sloped down to the creek. Though they could not hear its brawling voice, they could see the silvery shimmer of the water as it broke over rocks that were ebony-hued in the shadows.

Gerard stood with his hands jammed in his pockets, his entranced gaze on the breath-taking view before him.

"What a glorious sight!" he said softly after a moment. "I had no idea there were such mountains this side of the Rockies."

"Oh, we're very proud of our Blue Ridge!" Juliet told him.

"And well you should be. A shame that people don't know about the town of Haleyville. What a summer resort it would make if only there were facilities to take care of summer visitors and a road to get here."

Juliet bristled and said sharply, "Now see here — "

Gerard grinned at her and said hastily, "Oh, put down that gun, ma'am. Both Grady and Steve have told me how you cherish the privacy and the isolation of Haleyville and how much you resent any outsiders trying to get in. I wouldn't dare try to persuade you that you are wrong."

"Thanks," said Juliet curtly, and added, "I went out to see Miss Sarah this morning."

"I know," Gerard answered. "I wanted to go with you but didn't want to intrude on your other calls. And, of course, I knew my car wouldn't take that mule track. Only a jeep could do it."

He looked down at her and added anxiously, "She's all right, isn't she?"

"She's fine," Juliet answered and, because she couldn't think of any easier way to do it, plunged immediately into what had to be said. "She is a bit upset because you are planning to uproot her."

Gerard scowled in surprise, and a touch of resentment was in his voice when he repeated, "Uproot her? Because I plan to take her back home with me? Well, of course I do. You don't think I'd go away and leave her here alone, do you?"

Juliet looked up and met his eyes.

"Not even if you knew that was what she wanted more than anything else in the world?" she asked quietly.

Uneasily he studied her and then asked, "You think that's what she wants?"

"I know it, because she told me so herself."

He scowled and turned once more toward the view spread out before them.

"But how can I, Julie, knowing she is all alone there? If she needed help there would be no way for her to call for it. If there was somebody living in the house with her — "

"That's what she doesn't want!" Juliet cut in swiftly. "There is a neighbor woman, who lives within a mile of her, who would jump at the chance to come and live with her, because she is unwelcome in her son-in-law's home and treated as a drudge. But Miss Sarah doesn't want anyone in the house with her. She told me that a long time ago."

"Oh, then you've talked with her about the necessity of having someone live with her."

"Not the necessity, Gerard; only the advisability of it," Juliet corrected him. "But she is so opposed to the idea that I didn't make a real point of it. After all, Miss Sarah is a woman with a good mind of her own. She has lived alone in that little cabin ever since her father died years ago. It's the only real home she has ever known."

She broke off, slight abashed, as she saw the tightening of his jaw.

"I'm sorry, Gerard. I didn't mean to remind you that she was pretty unhappy the few years she was away from here. That was no fault of yours, as we both know. But you should realize that it must have been pretty bad for her to be willing to run away from a baby she adored and that she has grieved over for years. So how could you possibly want her to go back to a life like that again?

"But it wouldn't be like that now, Julie," Gerard insisted stubbornly. "Now that I understand, as I know Dad never could — "

"I understand exactly how Miss Sarah feels, Gerard, because it's the way I feel," Juliet told him. "I could never leave Haleyville, the mountains. This is my home, and the three years I spent in training in Atlanta were the most miserable of my life. And I didn't have snooty servants or guests who looked down their noses at me. I only had a very strict supervisor of nurses and some doctors and interns to collide with. But I hated every single moment I spent in a big city; and I don't ever want to leave Haleyville again, Gerard."

"Not even if you fell in love with what the mountain people call a 'flat-land furriner' and married him?" His tone was lightly teasing, but the look in his eyes was not, and beneath his gaze a soft fan of color touched Juliet's cheek.

"I can't imagine ever falling in love with a 'flat-land furriner'," she told him quietly.

For a moment their eyes met and clung. In his was a plea whose intensity startled her and made her heart beat faster. But in her own eyes he saw only the death of any faint hope he might ever have held that he could hope to win her.

"Not ever, Julie?" he asked at last.

"Not ever," she insisted, her tone steady.

He managed a mirthless grin.

"Poor Steve!" he said barely above his breath.

Juliet caught her breath on a small, soundless gasp.

"Why 'poor Steve'?" she countered after a moment.

Gerard grinned wryly.

"Oh, I got the impression he had some hopes of persuading you to move to Atlanta," he drawled.

"I'm sure you're quite wrong about that," Juliet told him curtly. "He knows very well that nothing else in the world is farther from my intentions."

Gerard was studying her thoughtfully.

"Come to think of it, I did hear something about you and Grady Alden, didn't I?" he mused aloud. "You are engaged?"

"Yes."

"And he's going to stay right here in Haleyville the rest of his life, so you two can grow old together in a town you are determined is not going to grow a single inch?" There was censure in Gerard's tone, and it made Juliet bristle slightly.

"I'm afraid I don't care to discuss that," she said coldly. "What Grady and I do is strictly our own business. What we are discussing is Miss Sarah and her desire to stay where she is, and your determination to uproot her."

"My determination to do what's best for her, Julie. You should know that's what I want: whatever is for her best interests, nothing more nor less."

"Then you'll go away and leave her just as you found her, because that's what she wants above all things!" Juliet assured him implacably.

Gerard looked down at her, and then he turned once more and surveyed the scene before him, and she saw that his jaw was set and hard.

"Just like that, eh? You're very sure you know what's best for everybody, aren't you, Julie?" His tone was faintly touched with acid.

"I'm sure that Miss Sarah knows what she wants and that she should be allowed to have exactly that," Juliet insisted stubbornly, and added more gently, "I know that you are fond of her — "

"Fond of her?" he cut in as though he resented the phrase. "Are you forgetting that she is my mother?"

"Of course not. And I know it must have been a great shock to you when you discovered that she was alive and came and saw her," Juliet answered him. "And

I can't help feeling that you and she both would have been better off in the long run if Steve Hayden had minded his own business and kept out of all this."

A glint of anger showed in Gerard's eyes.

"But he was minding his own business. As a newspaperman, he could not have hoped to discover material for a better story, no matter what it may have done to Miss Sarah and to me."

"She asked me, Gerard, to talk to you. To try to convince you that she wanted to stay right where she is, where she has lived all her life except for those few years with your father and you. I am only saying to you what she asked me to say."

"But you agree with her." His tone made it a statement, not a question, but Juliet answered as though it had been a question.

"I couldn't agree with her more," she answered, and went on quickly, "You see, I've known her so much longer than you have. I understand her and her needs and her wishes and her hopes; things you couldn't hope to understand in the little time you've been here and have known her."

"I suppose you are right," he said at last. "But, Julie, she is not only my mother. She is Mrs. Gerard Davison Senior, a very wealthy woman."

Juliet's smile was faintly touched with derision.

"And about that I'm sure she couldn't care less," she told him flatly. "She's been Miss Sarah Smithwick for so many years that I wonder she ever answered to Mrs. Davison."

He nodded as though he hated to admit that, yet knew that it was true.

"I'll never know an easy moment if I go off and leave her here the way she is now, all alone and so far out there that only a jeep can get to her," he burst out at last.

"And she'll never know an easy moment if you drag her away," Juliet insisted.

"Drag her away?" He obviously resented the phrase.

"That's the only way you could get her to go," Juliet insisted: "by forcing her. And you wouldn't want to do that, I know, would you?"

"Of course not."

Juliet said carefully, after a long moment of uneasy silence, "Then it's all settled?"

"Nothing's settled. I've got to do a lot of thinking before I can decide on anything," Gerard told her harshly.

Juliet sighed and lifted her hands in a little gesture of dismissal.

"Then I'd better get back to the clinic, in case I'm needed," she told him. "Are you coming?"

Gerard shook his head, his hands jammed deep into his pockets, looking at the scene spread out before him. The dying sunset was spilling a last golden radiance on the far-flung mountain ranges, though a mellow dusk already enclosed the valley below, and the glistening water of the creek could not be seen at all.

"Not just yet, Julie," Gerard said over his shoulder. "But thanks, Julie, for everything."

"I just hope I've been able to make you see what Miss Sarah wanted you to see," Juliet told him.

"Oh, I think you have, Julie," he answered curtly. "But I'm thanking you for the years of service you've given Miss Sarah." She was touched by his use of the name, which heretofore he had avoided.

"We love her, Gerard, all of us who know her. We'd do anything for her that we could, any time."

"Thanks. That's good of you."

His tone now was quite formal, and he did not turn his head to look at her as she walked away from him back up the path toward the clinic.

Grady came to meet her as she emerged from the path. The clinic's lights were glowing through the dusk, a haven for the sick and hurt and weary that might need the services the clinic so freely offered.

Grady looked worried as he greeted her.

"Dr. Laura said you'd gone for a

walk with Gerard Davison," Grady said. "Where is he?"

"Oh, I left him down at the Wishing Rock," Juliet answered. "He's trying to make up his mind about something."

Grady burst out anxiously, "Now, Julie, I hope you didn't try to discourage him. It will be a wonderful thing for Haleyville. And he really wants to do it, to show his appreciation to the town his mother loved so much she ran away from his father to come back here."

Juliet stared at him, puzzled and faintly apprehensive.

"I don't know what you're talking about, Grady," she told him. "Miss Sarah asked me to try to help her convince him that she doesn't want to leave here.

Grady looked enormously pleased.

"Oh, that's great! That's just great! Now he's sure to carry out his plans."

"What plans?"

"Oh, to give Haleyville a boost — to do some building; widen the roads; bring Haleyville into the center of things. He expects to begin with a fine modern motor court and a new hotel and an industry or two. All of it will give work to the men here who need it and bring new people into town.

He broke off, because even in the gathering dusk he could see her expression of acute distaste. Then he said sternly, "Now, Julie, don't you go off halfcocked and try to spoil things. I know, we all know, just how much you hate any kind of change. The good Lord knows we've all listened to you sounding off ever since you came back from Atlanta. You've fought against everything that could help the town grow. Well, now we've got a man who is rich enough to do some of the many things that have been needed here for years; and don't you go trying to talk him out of it, either!"

Anger sent sparks of green fire into Juliet's eyes and lent force to her voice as she cried out, "I have no intention of trying to talk him out of anything except dragging Miss Sarah away from here. She doesn't want that, and I'll do everything I can to prevent it from happening! But anything else he or the newly formed Chamber of Commerce wants to bring to Haleyville is your own business, just as the crime and the evil forces the changes will bring is your own business."

"Oh, for Pete's sake, Julie, don't be such a Gloomy Gus!" Grady protested in a tone he had never used to her before. "This is the chance Haleyville has needed ever since Old Man Healy moved down here from the gold rush country, set up a perpendicular farm for himself and his seven sons and fought tooth and nail to keep anybody else from moving in."

Juliet drew a long, hard breath, her hands tightly clenched in fists. Her eyes met his, and her tone was low and slightly unsteady with the fury she felt within her.

"All right, have your fine new Haleyville, if you can get him to build it for you. It might help your political ambitions. You know how I feel, so I am not going to waste any more breath arguing. If you've all made up your minds, and you've talked Gerard into spending a fortune doing all the things you're planning, that's just fine and dandy. Hooray for you!"

She brushed past him, her head high, and started on across the drive. Grady followed her, caught up with her at the steps and caught her hand in his, tightening his clasp when she tried to wrest her hand free.

"Now, Julie," his voice was anxiously coaxing, "don't run away mad. Can't you see what all this will mean for us — for you and me? Why, Julie we can get married before the summer is over. Gerard has appointed me his business manager for the whole project, and there will be a salary and commissions. Why, Julie, we can have a new house and all sorts of things."

Julie wrenched her hand free of his grasp and tilted her head defiantly.

"Well, thanks a heap, Grady, but I don't think I'd care to be married this summer, or any other summer. Not to you, anyway!"

There was a startled moment in which she realized that she had not meant to say that. The words had simply tumbled out against her will.

For a moment, there in the soft summer dusk, Grady stared at her as though he could not be quite sure he had really heard the words. And then, after a stunned moment, he repeated, "Not to me? Julie, are you trying to say that we are no longer engaged; that you aren't going to marry me, after all the years when we have planned to?"

And Julie said rashly, "I'm afraid that's exactly what I am saying, Grady."

Shocked amazement was replaced on Grady's face by a dawning fury.

"But, Julie, that's outrageous. You can't possibly mean it!" he protested hotly. "We've always planned to be married as soon as I was able to take care of you. And now that I'm going to be able, you break it off. Surely you aren't being so unreasonable as to end our engagement just when I'm about to be in a position to marry you?"

By now the sense of the words Juliet had flung at him, almost without realizing what she was saying, had crystallized into a firm conviction. She knew an odd, secret sense of relief at the thought that she was no longer bound by any understanding to Grady.

"Let's just say, shall we, that somehow I seem to have lost interest in getting married?" she told him coolly.

Grady's jaw set hard, and he looked more than ever like a young Abe Lincoln as he glared down at her.

"Especially to me?"

"If you want to put it like that."

"Then by all means let's put it like that," he told her harshly. "If you change your mind — "

"I won't."

"You can get in touch with me," said Grady loftily, went plunging back to his car and drove away with an angry spurting of gravel.

Juliet watched with a curiously detached

feeling as the car raced down the drive and turned into the road that led to Haleyville. She had the oddly pleasant feeling of being completely free. For the first time in years, she no longer looked ahead to a time when she would be Mrs. Grady Alden. And in that detached moment of freedom, she realized that she had never been really in love with Grady; not enough for marriage, anyway. He had simply been a sort of habit. She had grown up with him; she had been 'his girl' so long that now she felt somehow as though shackles had fallen from her. She laughed to herself at the absurdity of the thought as she turned and went into the house.

Dr. Laura looked up from her charts as Juliet entered the office and smiled at her.

"I hope Grady's staying for supper," she said lightly. "Gerard, too, if he cares to."

"Grady's gone, and I'm sure Gerard has other things on his mind," Juliet answered, and went on before her mother could speak, "Matter of fact, Grady's gone for good, permanently."

Dr. Laura asked anxiously. "Oh, Julie, you didn't quarrel with him?"

"I'm afraid I did," said Juliet, entirely without apology or even a trace of regret. "How would you feel about being stuck with an old maid daughter, Dr. Laura?"

Dr. Laura smiled, but the smile did not quite wipe out the anxiety in her eyes.

"Oh, I'm not worrying about that for a while," she answered. "You and Grady will make up."

"I don't really think so, Mother," Juliet countered slowly, a frown drawing her brows together as she sought to clear up her thoughts. "Somehow, I suddenly seem to realize that Grady and I are not really in love. It's just been force of habit that's kept us going together all these years. As long as I knew the possibility of our being married was somewhere off in the future, I thought it was going to be all right. But when he started talking about our being married before the summer was over, I suddenly seemed to see things much more clearly. I suppose it is possible to go along for years with one thought in mind, and then all of a sudden to realize that you don't really want what you've been planning for?"

"Oh, yes, I think it's quite possible," Dr. Laura answered as carefully as though Juliet had been a patient who had come to her for advice. "But I can't believe it's really happened to you and Grady."

"It has," Juliet answered, and there was a depth of conviction in her voice that startled Dr. Laura. "At least to me it has. And I'm sure Grady will realize it, too, now that his most cherished ambition seems to be about realized."

Mattie called them to supper, and Dr. Laura stood up and dropped her arm about Juliet's shoulder and gave her a little hug.

"Oh, well, you'll have plenty of time to think it over, and if you want to change your mind — " she began.

"Oh, sure, I can get in touch with

him. He reminded me of that," Juliet answered as they walked into the kitchen, to a table spread and waiting for them. Mattie was at the stove, smiling a white-toothed welcome that split her ebony face into a happy smile, as they took their places.

"Mist' Grady ain't comin' to supper?" she asked.

"Mist' Grady is a very busy young man, Mattie, and I doubt if he'll be dining with us for some time," Juliet informed her.

Mattie planted her fists on her ample hips, and the smile was swallowed up by a look of dark anxiety.

"You ain't been fussin' with Mist' Grady, is you, honey?" she demanded.

Juliet considered that thoughtfully for a moment, and then she grinned at Mattie and said cheerfully, "I suppose I have, Mattie."

"You bein' very foolish, honey!" Mattie scolded her as she slipped a piping hot squash patty on Juliet's plate, and its mate on Dr. Laura's. "Mist' Grady a fine young man. And, Miss Julie honey, he just about the only young man in these parts ain't got a steady girl friend. Don't you forget that!"

Juliet grinned at her.

"I won't, Mattie. I promise I won't forget it," she mocked lightly.

Mattie eyed her sternly.

"Well, now you see you don't, honey. You too pretty to be a old maid, and iffen you let your young man get away from you — " Juliet nodded demurely and went on with her supper.

"What we gonna do with her, Miss Laura?" Mattie asked.

Dr. Laura eyed Juliet with a deep affection that could not quite conceal the faint trace of anxiety in her eyes.

"I think the only thing we can do with her, Mattie, is to love her and do our best to understand her, don't you?" she asked.

"Well, yessum, I reckon so," Mattie answered, but without a great deal of conviction.

8

DURING the next few weeks, Juliet went about her rounds with anger in her heart. However, the anger was somewhat lessened by the happiness she saw on the faces of the townspeople. She heard eager chatter about jobs from some of the men who needed them badly; was aware of newcomers to town who brought new life to Main Street and who began building small cottages along the side streets that until then had been only paths.

She grew accustomed to encountering on Saturday afternoons women and girls wearing short shorts, Capri pants and halters and to men in Bermuda shorts; things that Haleyville had never before seen and that still left the older people shocked and appalled. But the younger ones welcomed the styles with such joy that Cofer Bros. General Store had to order them in quantity, and the items were sold out almost before they were unpacked.

But it was the road to Miss Sarah's that startled Juliet the most. The first morning she had started out on her rounds and had found a group of men working the road, widening what had been just a makeshift mule track, she had jerked the jeep to a startled halt. One of the workmen had come to the side of the jeep, grinning happily.

"Hi, Miss Julie. Reckon you're mighty glad to see something being done to this old pig track of a road. Reckon all of us out in these parts are mighty glad that Miz' Davison lives out here so's her son decided to fix the road. And out of his own pocket, too! Ain't that something — him finding he's got a Maw all along when he was thinkin' she was dead; and your Miss Sarah Smithwick turning out to be Miz' Davison, with a sight o' money of her own? You reckon she keeps it there in that cabin of hers?"

Juliet stiffened and her eyes flashed, but there was a pang of fear in her heart. If the word got around that Miss Sarah might have money hidden about the place, what unimaginable terrors might it bring down on her?

"I don't think anything of the kind, Sam Logan," she said more sharply than she had meant to speak. "Miss Sarah has never had more than a few dollars at one time in her life, and I'm quite sure her recently discovered son has too much sense and too much consideration for her to load her down with a lot of cash for her to keep here, even if she was foolish enough to do it. And we all know that Miss Sarah isn't foolish, don't we?"

"Well, sure, Miss Julie!" Sam agreed. "If they's anything we know about Miss Sarah, it's that she's a mighty smart and knowledgeable lady."

"Good!" said Juliet with frank relief. "I hope you'll spread the word around, Sam. We don't want to expose Miss Sarah to the danger of being robbed or attacked by somebody looking for whatever money she may have hidden, when we both know that she doesn't have any."

The man drew back, obviously deeply resentful.

"Now you looky here, Miss Julie. You know all of us folks up here. You and Dr. Laura — why, you've knowed us all our lives. You think there's any low-down, good-for-nothin' in these parts that would bother Miss Sarah?" he protested.

"No, Sam, I don't think any of the local people would," Juliet told him quietly. "What worries me is all these new people coming in. We don't know what kind of people some of them are. When you bring in strangers to a town like Haleyville, you have no way of checking on them, and some of them might be the kind that wouldn't know or respect Miss Sarah and would be thinking only that it might be profitable to rob her."

Still not quite mollified, Sam studied her intently.

"Reckon that's the reason you ain't been wanting Haleyville to start growing, ain't it, Miss Julie?" he suggested with a shrewdness that did not surprise Juliet too much.

"It's part of the reason, Sam," she answered. "I'm concerned not only about Miss Sarah. There are other people who live in isolated cabins who might seem likely prospects to the wrong sort of newcomers."

Sam considered that thoughtfully, and then he nodded reluctantly.

"Reckon there's a heap in what you say, Miss Julie," he agreed. "Reckon we'll all of us just have to be mighty on our guard with these strangers moving in."

"Will it be all right if I go on now, Sam? Can I get through to Miss Sarah? I'm due back at the clinic very soon," Juliet asked.

Sam stepped back and motioned to the men ahead to let her through. Juliet thanked him and nodded at the men, who moved back, grinning shyly at her. All were local people, she told herself with relief. They were Halevville people who knew and respected Miss Sarah; people with whom Miss Sarah would be safe.

She parked the jeep where it would be as little in the way of the workmen as possible, took out her worn black bag and started up the path. In sight of the cabin, she stopped short, wide-eyed. For a group of men were busily erecting a new cabin beside the path, well within sight of Miss Sarah's cabin.

They were strangers to her, and while they glanced curiously at her as she went past, they did not speak, nor did she. By the time she reached Miss Sarah's cabin, she was frowning and very uneasy. But her first sight of Miss Sarah, as that beaming lady swung open the door, did a lot to allay her uneasiness.

"Come in, come in, Julie! My, it's nice to see you, and to thank you for whatever you said to Gerry. It sure did the trick! Come on out on the back porch. Nettie and me are shelling peas to be canned." Miss Sarah ushered her out through the cabin and to the back porch, where Nettie Hicks sat, in her lap a big dishpan into which she was shelling peas.

"Why, hello, Nettie," Juliet greeted her. "It's nice to see you. Your health is so good I rarely ever get a chance to see you. I do hope the family is well?"

Nettie, a big-boned woman without an ounce of extra flesh, lifted her weathered face, and behind her steel-rimmed glasses her eyes sparkled.

"You ought to know they're fine, Miss Julie, or they'da been yelling for you or Miss Laura a long time ago," she replied. "Me, I'm just fine, thank the Lord, and happier'n I ever been in my life. Did you see the men-folks building me a cabin down the path?"

Miss Sarah had unbuttoned her cuff and rolled up her sleeve, and Juliet was taking her blood pressure while Miss Sarah beamed happily at Nettie, who smiled back even more radiantly.

"Your cabin?" Juliet repeated, when she had set down the figures and Miss Sarah was rolling down her sleeve.

"Gerry's building it for her, Julie," Miss Sarah reported eagerly. "Seems like he just couldn't make up his mind to leave me up here like I've been all these years. Seems like he just couldn't go without knowing that I could get help if I needed it. Wasn't that kind of him?"

Juliet stared at her and then at Nettie, and could not keep back the words: "But, Miss Sarah, you told me yourself — " She set her teeth and did not complete the sentence. Nettie and Miss Sarah both laughed and exchanged warm, affectionate glances.

"You mean Sarah told you she didn't want me here with her, talking her head off?" Nettie chuckled. "Well, you don't have to be bashful about that, Miss Julie. Me and Sarah has had a good, heart to heart talk and come to a firm understanding. Me being here in the cabin with her would sort of crowd her, seein's there's only one bed. Neither one of us wants to share a place as small as this. It's just fine for one person, but it sure would be crowded if they was two of us in it, specially one that likes to talk the way I do. Sarah, she told her boy how she felt, and he said he'd just build me a place of my own. Think of it, Julie — a place of my own!"

There was a soft glow in her eyes that lit up her weathered face and made her look years younger than the age Juliet knew was her real one.

"Gerry thought it would be just fine if Nettie and me could be close enough to be neighborly but not close enough to get in each other's hair," Miss Sarah explained. "So we got it all fixed. When I want to see Nettie, or if I need her for anything, I just hang a checked dishcloth out on the front porch."

"And I'll come a-runnin'," Nettie chimed in eagerly. "Times she wants to be by herself, like she's been for so many years, I'll stay away. I kinda think it's going to be right nice for me to have some time to myself, too, now and then."

She looked up at Juliet and added

earnestly, "I love my folks, Miss Julie. But sometimes when the young-'uns got to hollering and screaming, and their Maw and Paw got to quarreling, I sure wished I had me a little place where I could go off and be by myself nice and quiet. And now Miss Sarah's boy's giving me one. I have to keep pinching myself to believe it's all going to be true."

"I'm so glad for both of you," Juliet told them sincerely.

"My boy's really a fine boy, isn't he, Julie?" asked Miss Sarah pridefully.

"He really is, Miss Sarah. He's doing a lot for Haleyville, and I'm sure everybody is very grateful," said Juliet as she snapped the bag shut and turned to go. "That improvement on the road is going to make things easier for the summer visitors who want to see the scenery, too."

Miss Sarah's happiness was faintly clouded.

"Well, yes, I s'pose so," she admitted. "That's the only thing Gerry's doing that I don't like too much. Oh, he reminded me it would make it a lot easier for you to get out to see me, Julie, and that I'm proud about. But I feel it's going to bring some people I'm not going to want to see as much as I do you every week."

Juliet answered impulsively, "I suppose that's progress, Miss Sarah, and they tell me we can't stand in the way of progress."

Miss Sarah nodded. "That's what that nice Mr. Hayden said one day when he was out here."

Juliet stared down at her.

"That 'nice Mr. Hayden'?" she repeated incredulously. "You mean you have forgiven him for what he did to you?"

"Oh, not *to* me, Julie; *for* me," Miss Sarah corrected her gently. "He brought me and my boy together after all the years, when I didn't ever expect to see or hear anything about him except what I read in them New York newspapers. And I feel like that was a mighty fine thing. My boy thinks so, too. And none of it would have happened if it hadn't been for Mr. Hayden. Have you seen him lately?"

"No," said Juliet curtly, and started for the front door.

"Well, when he does come up, and I think maybe he will before long, you tell him I want to see him, Julie, and thank him," said Miss Sarah eagerly.

"I will, if I see him," Juliet answered.

Miss Sarah grinned at her, an almost impish gleam in her eyes.

"Oh, if he comes, you'll see him, Julie, if nobody else in town does. I'm sure of that," she answered lightly.

"Now, why would you say that, Miss Sarah?" Juliet's tone was brusque but she knew by the warmth in her face that her color had risen.

"Oh, I don't rightly know, Julie." Miss Sarah smiled. "I reckon he's mighty grateful to you and Dr. Laura for taking care of him that time he got hurt."

"That was our job, Miss Sarah. We'd have done as much for a stray dog that get hit by a car," Juliet answered sharply. She was instantly ashamed of herself, bade a hurried goodbye of Miss Sarah and went down the path to the waiting jeep.

So Miss Sarah thought Steve Hayden would be back, did she, and that he would make it his business to see Juliet? Remembering the last time she had seen him, Juliet wondered about that. But in her secret heart she knew, even though she would not admit it, that Miss Sarah was right. If or when Steve came back, he would see Juliet. And that he would be back she could not doubt. For he would certainly want to do a 'follow-up' series of articles on what had happened to Haleyville since the Davison story had appeared.

Well, let him come back, if he wants to. Juliet's mouth set in a thin, harsh line as she backed the jeep, turned it and headed for the clinic.

To her surprise, as she drove in and parked beneath the friendly old oak at the left of the neatly graveled drive, she saw a shining new car parked beside the oak. Grady Alden slipped out from behind the wheel and came to meet her, grinning a rather abashed grin.

"Hello, Julie," he greeted her, and

gestured toward the car. "How do you like the new bus? Isn't she a beauty — "

Julie blinked as she looked at the cream-colored hard top, chrome shining, pale green leather seats neatly covered by plastic, the whole thing looking as though it had just come off the showroom floor as, undoubtedly, it had.

"She really is a beauty, Grady," she answered him with surface pleasantness. "A very impressive car for a politician. It ought to help a lot when you start campaigning."

Grady flushed as though she had said something mildly offensive.

"Well, the old bus was about to fall to pieces, and repairs would have cost more than it was worth." He sounded apologetic. And then, as though he resented his attempt at an apology, he went on, "I've been waiting for you, Julie. There's something we have to talk about."

"Really?" Juliet's voice was mildly pleasant, touched with surprise. "I can't think what, Grady. I thought we had said all that needed to be said the last time you were here."

Grady's jaw set hard, and his eyes went cold.

"That's what I want to talk to you about, Julie," he told her. "You made it very plain that everything was over between us. Didn't you?"

"I certainly thought so," Julie told him coolly.

"Well, I met a girl over at the county seat last week — Rosemary Forbes. She's a very nice girl, and beautiful, too. Her father owns the bank over there. I think she likes me, a little anyway. But somebody has told her that I am engaged to you, and she won't date an engaged man. So I thought maybe you might help me to convince her that we're not engaged any more."

Julie's eyes danced a little, but she saw that he was so deeply in earnest that she had not the heart to tease him.

"Of course, Grady. I'd be glad to. What do you want me to do — give you a note telling her that our engagement is broken and that she may feel free to date you as often as she likes?" she suggested. And though she had not meant to tease him, she saw that he was offended at her words.

"Certainly not, Julie. Don't make fun of me," he snapped. "We've been friends a long time, and I hope we can go on being friends, no matter what happens. I just thought that maybe we might double-date with Rosemary, and you could let her know that our engagement is ended. Is that too much to ask?"

His tone was so stiff and so cold that Juliet felt a real touch of compunction and said instantly, "Of course not, Grady. I'll be glad to meet her. And I'm sure I can make it plain to her that the broken engagement was my fault, not yours. Because it was, Grady."

Grady looked deeply relieved.

"Well, yes, of course it was, Julie." He sounded so grateful that Juliet blinked a little and felt more than a trace of resentment. After all, she told herself indignantly, he didn't have to be all that grateful!

As though sensing her reaction, he went on hastily, "Oh, I don't want you to think, Julie, that I wasn't very much upset when you told me you had no intention of marrying me. I'd set my hopes and my plans on that and was glad I had this job with Davison because it seemed to me the perfect way to enable us to be married immediately. And when you told me you didn't want to marry me now or at any other time, it sort of knocked me for a loop."

"Until you met Rosemary." Juliet tucked the words in neatly, and Grady flushed.

"I met Rosemary a couple of months ago when I went into the bank with Davison, and she was there to take her father to lunch," he said stiffly. "The four of us went to lunch, and I liked her a lot, even at that first meeting. And I think she liked me. But at that time I was engaged to you, and of course I didn't make any effort to date her. But then when you said you didn't want to marry me after all, I did date Rosemary a few times. And then some gossip told her I was engaged to you and she wouldn't see me any more."

"I'm sorry, Grady, for any trouble I've caused you," Juliet told him with such obvious sincerity that the resentment vanished from his face and his eyes warmed.

"Then you'll double-date with us, Julie?" he asked eagerly.

"Of course," she answered. "Any time you say."

"Then how about tomorrow night, before Davison leaves? He'd like to share the double date, and I know you like him. How about it?" he asked eagerly.

"Why not? I think tomorrow would be fine," Juliet answered. "About six, don't you think, since it's a rather rough drive to the county seat, and we'll want plenty of time to drive it?"

Grady chuckled as he glanced lovingly at the new car.

"Oh, haven't you heard? The road over to the county seat has been worked on, and it's much better. They aren't going to pave it just yet, but they have widened it and put in a culvert over the creek, and this baby here just eats that road up. Six o'clock will be fine! I'll see you then. And thanks a lot, Julie, for everything."

"Think nothing of it, Grady," she answered, and watched as he drove away in the new car.

When she went into the clinic office, Dr. Laura looked up from her desk and smiled.

"What did you think of Grady's new car?" she asked. "He's as proud of it as a new father of a brand-new son," Dr. Laura commented. "I suppose you and he were patching up your quarrel?"

Juliet laughed as she put her worn black bag on a shelf.

"We patched up our quarrel," she answered lightly, "and I promised to double-date with him and his new girl friend tomorrow night so I could convince her that he and I were no longer engaged."

Dr. Laura's brows went up and she asked, startled, "Oh, does Grady have a new girl friend?"

Juliet nodded. "Isn't that wonderful?"

Dr. Laura studied her uneasily.

"Do *you* think so, darling?" she asked.

"Well, of course I do!"

Dr. Laura smiled with relief.

"Then so do I, darling." She asked, "Who is the new girl friend? Anybody we know? A Haleyville girl, I suppose?"

"Nope — she's Rosemary Forbes, daughter of the man who owns the bank at the county seat."

"Oh, the Forbes girl!" Dr. Laura said in surprise.

"Do you know her?"

"Yes. I've met her at the hospital a few times. She's a volunteer worker there; has been since she was sixteen. She's a lovely girl and a very nice one. Grady's in real luck!"

"That's good. So is she. Grady's quite a lad."

Dr. Laura studied her with more than a trace of anxiety in her loving eyes.

"You don't mind, darling?" she asked hesitantly.

"Mind?" Juliet laughed. "Why should I? I'm delighted for Grady!"

Dr. Laura heaved a deep sigh of relief.

"Then I'm delighted, too," she answered frankly. "I've never said anything before, honey, because I thought perhaps you were really in love with Grady. But now I know that he had just become a habit with you. That's the danger about young people 'going steady' for so long. They get so accustomed to each other that they believe they are in love. And, honey, that's not enough; not a sound basis for a successful and happy marriage."

"Isn't it, Mother?"

Dr. Laura smiled and shook her head.

"Not nearly enough, darling. It has to be a real love, deep and strong and able to withstand all the inevitable shocks and blows and disasters that come to every marriage, and that it takes a lot of very real love to survive."

Her tone was one of firm conviction. Juliet said gently, "Like what you and Dad had."

Dr. Laura nodded slowly, and there was a reminiscent tenderness in her eyes as she echoed, "Like Dad and I had. I don't ever want you to settle for anything less than that."

Juliet hugged her and pressed her cheek against her mother's and answered softly, "I won't, darling. I promise you I won't!"

"That's my girl!" said Dr. Laura. And as though to ease the tension of the moment, she added lightly, "And now Mattie's waiting to give us lunch; if we don't get it pretty soon, the first patients will be swooping down on us."

9

JULIET dressed carefully for the double date, and when Grady came for her she looked very fresh and pretty in a crisp honey-yellow linen frock that set off her shining hair and her green-gray eyes to perfection.

"Hey, you look scrumptious!" Grady used one of their old childhood phrases, and Juliet laughed and made him a slight, mocking curtsy.

"Why, thank you, kind sir." She laughed.

They stopped first at the hotel and picked up Gerard, who greeted Juliet with great warmth.

"Suppose you lead the way, Grady, and Julie and I will follow in my car," he suggested, "since your car and mine both are convertibles."

"Why not?" Juliet agreed, and let him guide her to his car, which was parked a little way down from the hotel's main entrance.

Grady waited for them at the Forbes'. As they mounted and crossed the white-columned verandah, the door was flung open by a radiantly lovely girl whose shining golden hair reached almost to her shoulders and was held back from her face by a blue ribbon band. Her dress was an embroidered blue organdie, and Juliet, being feminine, noticed that the hair band and the dress were the exact shade of the girl's lovely eyes.

She greeted them warmly, her eyes clinging to Juliet so closely that Juliet yearned to say, "Don't worry; he's yours if you want him."

"Hello, Rosemary," Grady greeted the girl, and there was a warmth in his voice that had never been there for Juliet. "This is Juliet. And of course you've met Gerard."

Rosemary gave Gerard an entrancing smile and turned to Juliet.

"I've met your mother, Dr. Laura, at the hospital," she said happily. "She's a wonderful woman. Everybody there adores her."

Juliet smiled at her. "And Mother says that you're pretty popular there yourself."

Rosemary made a slight deprecating gesture.

"Oh, I fetch and carry and do as I'm told, read to the children and try to cheer up the patients as much as they'll let me," she answered. "Grady, you and Gerard go on in the living room. Dad's waiting for you with cocktails or whatever you want. Julie and I will be down in a few minutes. I'm not quite ready to leave yet."

It wasn't at all subtle, Juliet admitted to herself with secret amusement as Rosemary urged her up the wide stairs and along to a bedroom overlooking a magnificent sweep of mountains, still bathed in the faint afterglow of the sunset.

When the door had closed behind them, Rosemary turned impulsively to Juliet and, her color high, asked flatly, "Do you hate me, Juliet?"

Juliet, touching fingers to her hair, that had been slightly disturbed by the drive from Haleyville, turned to her, startled.

"Hate you?" she repeated, uncomprehending.

"Because of Grady, I mean." Rosemary was as unsubtle about this as she had been about her desire to get Juliet away from the men for a private talk. "I didn't know he was engaged to you when I first met him. And then when I found out he was, I wouldn't date him any more, until he told me your engagement had been broken."

Juliet said lightly, "Well, stop worrying, Rosemary. Grady and I broke our engagement by mutual consent. It wasn't really an engagement; it was just a sort of understanding, one of those things you drift into when you've known each other since childhood and you get the habit of being together and mistake it for being in love. As soon as we both realized what it was, the only sensible thing seemed to be just to put an end to it. It was nobody's fault. I'm sure you understand, Rosemary, how those things happen."

Rosemary had dropped down into a brocaded slipper chair near the dressing table bench where Juliet sat. Now she put her hands to her eyes for a moment and drew a long, deep breath of abject relief. Finally she dropped her hands and smiled tremulously at Juliet.

"I'm so glad, Juliet," she breathed, and her voice was not quite steady. "I was so afraid that after maybe meeting me, Grady had — well — "

"Decided to jilt me?" Juliet laughed, "Rosemary, you *are* a silly little goof!"

"Oh," protested Rosemary earnestly, "now that I've met you, seen you and know what a darling you are, I know no man would ever jilt you; certainly not for a feather-brain like me!"

"Rosemary, don't be silly," Juliet urged. "You are exactly the sort of wife a man like Grady would need and want. I'm not! And anyway, it's you he wants to marry; not me. So for goodness' sake, stop worrying about coming between us! You didn't, and I wish you both all the happiness in the world."

Rosemary studied her for a moment, and then she said thoughtfully, "Then it must be Gerard."

Puzzled, Juliet asked, "What must be Gerard?"

"That you're in love with, if not with Grady!"

Juliet stared at her, caught halfway between exasperation and anger.

"For heaven's sake, Rosemary, is there a law that says I have to be in love with one man before I break my engagement to another?" she protested.

"Well, no, I suppose not," admitted Rosemary. "But up here, where girls marry before they are out of their teens, some of them before they get into their teens, and where marriageable males are at such a premium, I always thought a smart girl didn't drop one before she was sure of another one."

Juliet laughed, but there was a faint edge to her laughter.

"You really *are* a goof, Rosemary," she protested. "I'm well out of my teens, and believe it or not, I'm not in the slightest hurry to trade my nursing career for marriage."

"And you're not in love with Gerard?"

"Certainly not!"

"Nor with Grady either?"

"Nor with Grady either!"

Rosemary studied her anxiously.

"Have I made you mad?" she asked.

"Oh, don't be so silly!"

Rosemary stood up, her smile radiant.

"I'm so glad," she said happily. "I'd love you to be my friend, Juliet. Will you be?"

"Of course," Juliet answered, and added, "Shouldn't we be going down? The boys will think we've deserted them."

"Of course," Rosemary answered, and added as they left the room, "Dad wanted us to have dinner here. He hates eating alone, and when he's at home, he likes me to bring my dates home for dinner. I hope you don't mind?"

"Of course not," Juliet assured her as

they went down the stairs.

There was the rumble of men's voices in the living room, and a masculine laugh as they crossed the hall and entered the room. The three men turned immediately, and Juliet saw a short, stout, middle-aged man she recognized as Justin Forbes, though she had never met him.

He came forward to greet Juliet, and Rosemary went straight to Grady, smiling up at him as she tucked her hand through his arm with a happy air of proprietorship that made him beam down at her. And then, above her shining golden head, he looked across at Juliet with a depth of gratitude in his eyes that told her how pleased he was that she and Rosemary had reached such a perfect agreement.

"I have just been saying to Gerard and Grady that I hope you won't mind having dinner here, Juliet," said Justin Forbes, smiling down at Juliet with friendly warmth. "Aside from the fact that I feel sure the food will be much better here than you could get in any of the roadside places, I am selfish about any guests that come near. I want to get to know them. And besides, I hate eating alone."

Juliet laughed. "I don't blame you, Mr. Forbes. It *is* a lonely business, isn't it? And I appreciate your hospitality!"

A middle-aged woman in a neat black uniform beneath a snowy starched white apron announced dinner, and Gerard offered his arm to Juliet, smiling at her as Grady and Rosemary followed.

The dining room was comfortably but not elaborately furnished, and the big oval table was laid with a shining damask cloth. A bowl of flowers from the garden was set in the center. The middle-aged woman, tight-lipped, silent-footed, served them deftly and withdrew.

Juliet looked about the table. Rosemary sat at the head, a gracious and experienced hostess, with her father opposite her and Grady at her right. Gerard sat opposite Juliet. As he met her eyes he gave her a warm smile, and Juliet felt the color rise in her cheeks as she returned the smile.

Justin said, "I understand you are leaving us tomorrow, Gerard, and I'm sorry to hear it."

"But he'll be back for the Harvest Festival at Haleyville," Grady said before Gerard could speak. "He has promised."

Gerard smiled at him and answered, "I wouldn't miss it for the world."

"Good!" said Justin heartily. "We'll look forward to seeing you then, won't we, Rosie?"

Rosemary gave Gerard a radiant smile. "Of course we will."

"We all will," said Grady.

"Thanks; you are all very gracious," Gerard said.

Later, when the evening was finished, Grady and Juliet drove back to Haleyville in Grady's cherished new car. They had said goodbye to Gerard at the hotel and heard again his promise to return for the Harvest Festival in late September.

As they drove away from the hotel, Grady chuckled and said musingly, "Boy, is he ever going to be surprised when he gets back and finds out it isn't a

Harvest Festival at all, but a Gerard Davison Day!"

Juliet looked at him, startled, and repeated, "A Gerard Davison Day!"

Grady nodded, his eyes on the steep incline of the newly widened road ahead of him.

"Haleyville wants to show its appreciation for all he has done for the town and its people, and we're really going to put on a show for him: fireworks, speeches, the works."

Uneasily, Juliet asked, "But do you think he'll like that?"

Grady chuckled. "No, I'm afraid he won't. That's why we're calling it a Harvest Festival, instead of letting him know what it's really going to be. He's just the sort of unassuming guy who might refuse to show up if he knew what we had in mind. But we owe it to him, Julie. And we want to do it, for our sake as much as for his. Gratitude needs to be publicly expressed in a case like this, don't you think?"

"Well, I suppose so, even at the cost

of his embarrassment," Juliet agreed reluctantly.

They had reached the foot of the steep incline, and Grady was able to take his eyes off the road long enough to glance down at her.

"You're not still angry about the changes in Haleyville, Julie?" he asked quietly.

"No, Grady," Juliet answered honestly. "I admit I hated having the place changed. It was so much what Steve called it: a sort of Shangri La; a place where you could come in and close the door and be quiet and peaceful. I resented outsiders coming in. But as Steve said, that was selfish of me. And now that I've seen what an improvement all this makes in the well-being of the Haleyville people — " She broke off and gave him a rueful grimace. "I sound downright pompous, don't I? I don't mean it: it's just that it's taken me a long time to realize just what all this means for Haleyville. And to think I was trying to keep them from getting it!"

"Steve will be relieved to know you feel that way," Grady told her. "I was talking to him the other day, and he asked if you still hated him."

"You were talking to him? He's been here? To Haleyville?"

Juliet did not realize how eager her voice sounded.

"No, I saw him over at the county seat," Grady answered, obviously curious about her excited eagerness. "I don't suppose he had time to come over to Haleyville. But he'll be here for the Festival. He promised to cover it for his paper."

"Well, of course, since he's the one who really started things, he should be here, shouldn't he?" Juliet's voice was flat now. "It should really be Steve Hayden Day, rather than Gerard Davison Day, don't you think? I'm sure Steve would love that!"

Grady chuckled. "I'm sure he would, but a fat chance he's got of getting it!" he answered, and plunged into an enthusiastic description of all the things planned for the Festival. The account lasted until he let Juliet off at home and drove away.

Juliet went quietly into the house and upstairs, careful not to arouse Dr. Laura as she let herself into her room and closed the door soundlessly.

She stood for a long moment just inside the room, in the darkness, invaded only by the soft flood of silver moonlight that spilled through the windows.

So Steve had been less than twenty miles away and hadn't even driven those few miles to say 'hello' to her.

She drew a deep breath, startled to realize how much her heart had sunk at the thought.

10

JULIET came back from her rounds one morning a week or two later to find a big white ambulance parked beside the drive and a tall, lean, suntanned young man climbing out of it.

He grinned at her, opened a book of sales slips and leafed through them, taking her in in her uniform, her cap perched atop her shining black hair. "Miss Juliet Cochran?" he asked. "Got a package for Dr. Laura Cochran, but I was told it would be all right for you to sign for it."

He held out the book to her, and Juliet signed the slip, asking, "You are using an ambulance to deliver a package?"

The man laughed. "Lady, the ambulance *is* the package. It's for the Haleyville clinic and Dr. Cochran and her nurse."

Thunderstruck, Juliet stared at him and then at the handsome, gleaming ambulance. Her breath caught and her eyes widened.

"An ambulance? For us?" she gasped.

"Compliments of a fellow named Gerard Davison; who else?" The man grinned. "Talk about out-of-season Santa Clauses, that man really qualifies, in my book!"

"But — but — " Juliet stammered, unable to take it all in.

Dr. Laura came hurrying out, anxious-eyed as she glanced at the ambulance.

"What is it, Julie? Who's been hurt and brought here instead of to the hospital?" she asked.

Juliet reached out and put an arm about her mother and said soothingly, though her voice was far from steady, "Nobody's been hurt, darling. It's our ambulance! Gerard gave it to us!"

Dr. Laura looked as stunned as Juliet had felt. For a moment, while the salesman watched them, grinning, enjoying their amazement, neither of them could speak.

The salesman at last broke the silence by asking, "Can you drive it, Miss Cochran? Dr. Cochran?"

"Well, of course I can," Juliet stammered. "So can Mother. We're used to a jeep, and on roads that were not improved until a few weeks ago. I can drive it, but I can't be sure it's really ours, or that all this is happening."

"To tell you the truth," confided the salesman, "that's about the way we felt at the agency when Mr. Davison came in and ordered it. We had to get it from Atlanta, of course, and it took a little time. But he wrote a check for it just as casually as I'd write one for the week's groceries. More so, to be honest about it. Sometimes, when I write such a check, I'm wondering if it will bounce. But I don't suppose any such thought ever occurred to Mr. Davison."

There was a distinctly wistful note in the man's voice, and then he once more became brisk and businesslike.

"Well, it's yours, ladies, and I'm sure it won't give you any trouble. But if it does, just call this number, and we'll be over in a jiffy to put it straight for you."

"Thanks," said Julie, and tucked the

card into her pocket.

"My pleasure," grinned the salesman, and added, "Would you like me to take you for a run, show you any of the little things you may not be familiar with?"

Juliet said quickly, "Suppose I drive you back to the county seat in it. You can show me anything I need to know, and I'll bring it back alone."

"Now that," said the salesman approvingly, "is a darned good idea. I'll be grateful for the lift, though I could probably bum a ride in the village."

Juliet managed a small, shaky laugh.

"Sir! How dare you call Haleyville a village? We're a town, and don't you forget it!"

The man made a slight, apologetic gesture, his eyes twinkling.

"How right you are, Miss Cochran. I've got some folks living around here, but I hadn't been over since last Christmas. When I drove in just now, I could hardly believe it was the same town. A motel, a good road from the county seat, new houses, some new stores on

Main Street. This town's really had a face-lifting! That guy Davison doesn't fool around when he starts something, does he?"

"He really doesn't," Juliet agreed heartily.

"He's a wonderful person," said Dr. Laura, her hand touching the side of the ambulance gently, as though it had been a small and delicate child that could be bruised by an incautious hand.

The salesman scowled. "Still, with the kind of money he's got, I suppose it's easy for him," he commented, and added hastily as Juliet and Dr. Laura stiffened, "Well, Miss Cochran, shall we get going?"

"Why not?" Juliet agreed. She slipped in behind the wheel and eyed the instrument panel with a wary eye.

"Be careful, honey!" Dr. Laura called anxiously as the ambulance slid down the drive and turned into the road leading through town and to the county seat.

The salesman at first watched Juliet closely as she drove. Then, as though convinced she knew what she was doing, he relaxed a little and looked at the crowds thronging Main Street, the gleaming new store-fronts, the big supermarket on the outskirts, its ample parking space well-filled with cars.

"Yes, sir," he mused as the ambulance slipped out of town, followed by interested glances from passersby, "Haleyville sure has had a face-lifting! Wouldn't surprise me if my boss decided to open an agency over here instead of expecting Haleyville people to come to hunt him up over at the county seat."

But Juliet was too absorbed in the task of familiarizing herself with the instrument panel to answer him.

By the time she returned to the clinic, she felt as if she had been driving the ambulance for ages and were as familiar with it as with the faithful old jeep.

Dr. Laura was waiting for her on the steps by the time she parked the ambulance and asked eagerly, "How does it handle, darling?"

"Like a dream, honey. You won't have

a bit of trouble with it, and neither will I!"

"Isn't it wonderful? Oh, Julie, what a lovely gift! You *do* think we ought to accept it, don't you?"

Juliet stared at Dr. Laura, her brows raised, a smile tugging at the corners of her mouth.

"Accept it? Are you out of your mind, honey?" she protested. "How could we give it back to him? You don't return presents to Santa Claus — and that's what Gerard Davison is to this whole area."

"No, of course not," Dr. Laura agreed, her eyes taking in the gleaming white car. "It's something I never dared dream we would have: a brand-new ambulance with all the latest gadgets and facilities for the care and comfort of a patient! We'll never be able to thank Gerard enough."

"Well, we'll have our chance to try at the Festival next week," Juliet comforted her. "It's going to be quite a Festival. Miss Sarah is all excited. I promised to come out and get her and Nettie and bring them in for the show."

"Don't you imagine Gerard will want to do that himself? After all, she is his mother."

"I know," Juliet agreed. "But from the plans Grady and the others are cooking up to entertain him, I don't imagine they're going to leave him much time for a drive out there, or anywhere else except the town square."

"Does Miss Sarah know that the real purpose of the Festival is to honor Gerard?" asked Dr. Laura as they went into the house and she paused at the steps to look back with shining eyes at the ambulance.

"No, I thought it might be better if she didn't know," Juliet answered, and hesitated. "I was afraid she might get over-excited. Or do you think I should tell her in advance?"

Dr. Laura considered the matter thoughtfully for a moment. "I don't think you should. Of course, the anticipation of attending the Festival, after all the newspaper stories about her really being Mrs. Davison Senior, has more or less accustomed her to excitement. And I don't suppose seeing the town festooned with banners reading 'Welcome to Gerard Davison Day' will be a shock to her. It will probably make her so happy that she'll forget she was ever shy and retiring."

"Maybe you're right," Juliet agreed, and gave a small chuckle. "I think the one who is going to be shocked is Gerard himself. He's coming here thinking it's merely an annual Harvest event, when the trees are so beautiful that people come for miles to enjoy the mountain scenery and Haleyville puts on a show to welcome them. Then he'll find it's a day in his own honor."

Dr. Laura laughed, too. "I hope there will be somebody behind him so he can't cut and run back to the county seat and away from the celebration. I don't think he's going to enjoy being heaped with honors and hearing speeches that will probably be more like eulogies, will he?"

"I'm afraid not," Juliet agreed. "But there's no way to rescue him now. The town would never forgive us."

Dr. Laura asked her, "You have gotten over your aversion to the changes in Haleyville, darling?"

Juliet considered that for a moment, and then she met her mother's lovingly anxious eyes.

"Yes, I think I have," she answered slowly. "At least I've begun to realize all that the changes have meant for the people here, and to agree that I was being selfish in wanting Haleyville to stay just as it was."

"I'm so glad, darling," said Dr. Laura.

"So am I," Juliet admitted honestly.

They smiled at each other in affectionate understanding.

As they walked into the house, Juliet asked before she could check the impulse, "Did you know Steve was in town a few days ago?"

Dr. Laura looked at her in surprise.

"And he didn't stop in to say 'hello'?" she marveled.

"He wasn't here in Haleyville. He was over at the county seat. Grady saw him there."

"Oh," said Dr. Laura, and gave Juliet a swift, anxious glance, "then I suppose he was too busy to drive over. But he will be here for Davison Day, I'm sure."

"I suppose so," Juliet agreed without emphasis.

Dr. Laura's eyes were slightly worried as she looked at Juliet. But she held back any comment she might have made, and the moment passed.

The next few days were busy ones, both for Haleyville and for the clinic. School would be opening soon, and children were being brought in for checkups and for treatment for various illnesses and accidents. In addition, Juliet was busy getting her out-patients settled in for the winter.

All over town, banners went up with Gerard's name on them. A speaking platform was set up beside the town square, facing the creek and the Confederate monument. People were meeting in little groups to discuss the festivities planned to honor the man who had brought all this unexpected but deeply appreciated progress and prosperity to Haleyville.

Juliet was not surprised, when she called on Miss Sarah a few days before the date of the Festival, to discover that Miss Sarah knew the real purpose of the celebration.

Her eyes sparkling, Miss Sarah said eagerly, "Nettie's son took her to town for our grocery shopping yesterday, and she came back reporting that Gerard's name was up all over town and that it isn't really going to be a Harvest Festival after all. It's really to be a day in honor of my son!"

Juliet smiled as she put the blood pressure gauge back in its nest in her black leather bag and snapped the bag shut.

"That's right, Miss Sarah. I was going to tell you, but I thought maybe we could keep it for a surprise," she answered.

"Oh, it was a surprise." Miss Sarah glowed happily. "Why, when Nettie told me, I could scarcely believe it. But she insisted it was so. And she'd brought me one of the cards that the supermarket had in its window, with Gerard's picture on it and big black letters saying, 'Welcome, Gerard Davison.'"

She proudly drew Juliet to the wall above the stand that held the scrapbook in which Steve Hayden had discovered the truth about her and Gerard. She had thumb-tacked the card proudly to the wall, so that Gerard smiled down at them.

"It's not really a very good picture, is it, Julie?" Miss Sarah worried. "He's a lot better looking than that, isn't he?"

Juliet smiled at her. "He really is, Miss Sarah. But then pictures rarely do people justice."

"Well, no, I guess not," Miss Sarah replied. She put out a gnarled hand and touched the picture lovingly as though to apologize for having found any fault at all with it.

"Well, I'll drive out and pick you and Nettie up, Miss Sarah, in time for you to be part of the welcoming committee Tuesday morning," Juliet promised as she prepared to leave.

Miss Sarah looked startled.

"Oh, no, Julie, I couldn't!"

"Come now, Miss Sarah. It's going to be a great day for Gerard."

"I bet he'll hate folks thanking him and making a fuss over him."

"It could well be that you are right, Miss Sarah," Juliet agreed. "But he'll want you to be there, to stand beside him. It may be an ordeal for him, and it will help him if you are with him."

Miss Sarah said slowly, "It's been so long since I've been where there are people, Julie. And there'll be an awful crowd there, I know."

"Well, Grady and the others who have worked so hard on this Day will be terribly disappointed if there are not crowds of people," Juliet reminded her. "You were perfectly willing to go to the Festival. You and Nettie seemed very pleased when I offered to come out for you."

"That was different," Miss Sarah protested. "At the Festival, folks wouldn't be staring at me and pointing me out and making a fuss over me. They'd be busy with the Festival; not with Gerard and me."

"That's quite true, Miss Sarah," Juliet answered. "And you needn't come unless you really want to. I know Nettie will want to be there. I can come out and get her, and if you've changed your mind by then and want to come with us, you can. How's that?"

Miss Sarah beamed with unashamed relief.

"Oh, that'll be just fine, Julie. That'll be just fine!" she answered.

"Good. Then I'll see you Tuesday morning, Miss Sarah," Julie told her before she left the house and went briskly down the drive toward the jeep.

Nettie was waiting for her on the front steps of the neat little cabin that was now her pride and joy.

"How's Miss Sarah this morning, Miss Juliet?" she asked.

Juliet paused and looked at her in surprise.

"You don't know? You haven't seen her this morning?" she asked.

Nettie waved a hand toward Miss Sarah's cabin and said, a faint trace of belligerence in her voice, "You don't see any checked rags hanging out up there, do you? She made it awful plain that unless she hangs out a checked dishrag, I ain't supposed to show myself."

"Well, yes. But if anything happened to her in the night, if for some reason she couldn't get out to hang out a dishrag to summon you — "

Nettie grinned. "Well, don't let this on to her, Miss Juliet. But soon's I get up, I sneak up there and have a look around. Most times she's in the kitchen, happy as a cricket and stepping around right smart, and I just sneak back down here without letting her know I've seen her. Reckon she wouldn't like it too much if she knew I was sort of spying on her. She was up crack o' day this morning, bustling about, doing her housekeeping chores. I was just wondering what she's going to do 'bout going into Haleyville for Davison Day."

"She hasn't decided yet," Juliet answered. "I'll come out for you Tuesday morning, and if she wants to go with us, she can."

"Oh, that'll be just fine!" Nettie said happily. "And she'll be ready to go, I betcha a pretty. Be mighty foolish for her to miss a thing like that, wouldn't it?"

"I suppose it would, Nettie. I'll see you Tuesday morning about nine-thirty," Juliet answered, and went on to her jeep.

11

DAVISON DAY dawned gloriously, as though the weather were trying to do its part toward making it a perfect occasion. All the mountains were clothed in their most fantastic colors, and the little creek had never been so busy or singing so cheerfully.

The barbecue pits were already giving off a savory fragrance by sunrise, and the men tending them were boasting of the excellence of the midday dinner that was going to be served at the long tables beneath the trees just beyond town as soon as the 'speechifying' was over. In kitchens all over the area, women were bustling about, preparing huge bowls of salad, icing cakes, adding their own very important touches to preparations for that 'dinner on the grounds' that was always a very important part of Festival day.

Juliet was delighted when she reached Miss Sarah's cabin and found her dressed in the 'city-bought' clothes Gerard had provided for her when he had first thought she would accompany him back to New York.

"So you decided to go, Miss Sarah. I'm so glad," Juliet told her as she guided her carefully down to the jeep, where Nettie was already waiting.

"Well, I reckon I couldn't let him go through this all by himself seeing it was him coming here to find me that set the whole thing off," Miss Sarah admitted. There was an unaccustomed tinge of pink in her face, and her voice was touched with eagerness.

"He'll be very glad to see you there, Miss Sarah!" Juliet assured her as she turned the jeep about and headed back for town.

Long before they reached Haleyville, they became enmeshed in a stream of unaccustomed traffic: pick-up trucks, ancient cars, even a horse and buggy or two. And when they reached Main

Street, the sidewalks were already lined with eagerly waiting people.

"Here they come! Here they come!" shouted somebody. And a motorcade came in view, led by Grady's car, bearing a United States Senator who had been born and had grown up near there and who wasn't averse to mending some political fences by being the speaker at such a festivity. Behind Grady's car came Gerard's, and Juliet felt a tinge of pity as she saw the dazed, bewildered look on his face as the people began to shout his name.

Obviously the whole thing had been a great shock from which he hadn't yet recovered. As his eyes swept the crowd, he saw the jeep, with Miss Sarah sitting proudly beside Juliet, tears of pride slipping down her cheeks.

Gerard threw up his hand to stop the motorcade, and all the cars behind him drew to a grinding halt. He leaped out of his car, came swiftly to the jeep, lifted Miss Sarah out in his arms and carried her to the front seat of his own car, where he put her down as gently as though afraid she might break. A great roar went up from the crowd, there was a burst of hand-clapping, and Nettie frankly burst into tears as Gerard rejoined the motorcade, Miss Sarah seated proudly beside him.

"Now, wasn't that just the sweetest thing you ever seen, Miss Juliet?" Nettie sobbed. "He held up that whole parade just so's his Maw could ride with him. I reckon this is a day Miss Sarah ain't never going to forget!"

"I'm sure she isn't, Nettie!" said Juliet, and was aware of a mist of tears in her own eyes as she watched the cars drive past to the parking lot just beyond the speakers' stand.

When the cars had all been parked, and the U.S. Senator stood up to be introduced by Grady and then to make his speech, Nettie whispered to Juliet, "I promised I'd help with the dinner fixin's, Miss Juliet. I'll just trot along and help the others. I'm obliged to you for bringing Miss Sarah and me. And don't you worry none about us getting home. Somebody will be sure to be driving our way."

Juliet nodded, and Nettie moved off into the crowd. A moment later, a voice spoke beside the jeep, and Juliet turned, startled, to meet Steve Hayden's eyes. He was standing beside the jeep watching her, his attitude one of casual interest, though the look in his eyes was far from casual.

"Hello," he greeted her. "It's quite a day for Haleyville, isn't it?"

Juliet hoped her voice sounded steadier than her heart felt as she answered, "Quite a day. And you belong up there on the speakers' stand quite as much as Gerard Davison. Without you, none of this could ever have happened."

Steve eyed her warily.

"I'm not quite sure whether there's a knife concealed in that crack or whether you're on the level."

"I'm quite on the level," Juliet assured him. "Haleyville owes you quite a lot, and so do the Davisons."

"Then you don't still hate me for my snooping and prying and broadcasting the charms of Haleyville so that strangers moved in and are still moving in?"

Juliet shook her head and managed a smile that was not entirely steady.

"I don't hate you at all," she answered. "And I was a little hurt that you didn't stop in to say 'hello' to Mother and me when you were at the county seat a week or so ago."

"Oh, Grady told you I was there?"

Juliet nodded. "Dr. Laura said she supposed you were too busy to make the drive over here, even to find out what a good road we have now," Juliet told him.

"I wasn't too busy at all," Steve told her flatly "But I didn't know then that you and Grady had broken your engagement. And I couldn't see any point to coming over here and getting kicked in the teeth again by a girl who made no secret of the fact that she hated the sight of me and the sound of my voice. But now that I know you and Grady are no longer an item — " He looked about them and saw that the crowd was intent on the Senator's speech. He got into the jeep beside her. "Let's find a place where we can talk. There are a million things, by actual count, that you and I have to say to each other."

Juliet blinked even as she started the jeep. "There are?" she asked.

Steve gave her a look that barely missed being a glare and said curtly, "Well, half of them are things I have to say to you. The other half you can say to me. But in a little privacy, if you don't mind."

"Well, of course not. Privacy's very necessary sometimes," Juliet stammered idiotically, and hoped he could not hear the rapid, uneven pounding of her heart that seemed to be shaking her whole body.

"How right you are. And this is one of the times," Steve told her firmly.

Juliet turned the jeep's nose in at the entrance to the clinic and parked beneath the giant oak whose leaves were stubbornly refusing to fall, even though they had begun to turn color. "How is this?"

"Seems to me I remember something even better. Somebody will be coming along any minute with a bad case of the colliwobbles, and you'll have to treat them," said Steve firmly, and drew her with him down the path to the giant rock where she had stood with Gerard to talk about his mother and her wish to remain where she was.

When they reached the spot, Steve looked for a moment at the view and said half under his breath, "What a spot! It's something for a fellow to remember all his life, either as the spot where he found his greatest happiness or where he barely managed not to heave himself down the mountain-side because he realized he didn't have anything to live for."

Juliet stared at him, wide-eyed, and waited.

Steve looked down at her and jammed his hands into his coat pockets as though he could not trust them to remain free. His brows were drawn together in a scowl that indicated he was searching his mind for some way to lay before her what he wanted to say.

"Knowing how you feel about Haleyville, and that you would never want to leave," he began slowly at last, "I guess the first thing I ought to tell you is that I am moving to Haleyville. So you could marry me, if you liked the idea, and still not have to leave your beloved Shangri La."

Juliet gasped, "I could *what?*"

Steve's scowl deepened. "Is the idea that unattractive to you?"

"Well, no. But it's pretty unexpected."

"Oh, come off it," he scoffed roughly. "You've known all along that I was in love with you."

"How could I? You never said a word — "

"How could I, when you were engaged to Grady, and when you hated me so and all that I stood for? Think I wanted you to draw a gun on me for daring to say

I was in love with you? And anyway, I wasn't entirely sure until after I went away. And when I came back with Davison, you sure gave me the rough side of your tongue. You don't deny that, do you?"

"Well, no," she stammered.

"Then how could you expect me to let you know how I was beginning to feel about you?" he demanded.

"I couldn't, I suppose." Her voice was faint and her eyes were wide with incredulity that this could be really happening.

"Well, now that I know you and Grady have busted up, I have a chance to come to Haleyville and settle down. With you, it would be a real Shangri La, and I'd ask nothing better out of life. But without you, it wouldn't mean a thing. So I have to ask you to decide for me."

Juliet managed to ask, "Decide what?"

"Whether or not you'd be willing to marry the editor and publisher of the *Haleyville Clarion.*"

She stared at him, wide-eyed.

"You want to edit a small town weekly newspaper?" she gasped. *"You?"*

He looked mildly offended.

"You don't think I can do it?" he asked.

"Well, of course. It's just that I can't imagine you wanting to!"

"It's the lifelong ambition of two thirds of city newspapermen to have a small town newspaper that will be their own baby. But not many get the chance; not many are lucky enough to know Gerard Davison."

"Oh, he's going to buy the paper and give it to you?" Juliet did not realize that there was the faintest possible hint of censure in her voice. But Steve caught it, and the scowl returned in full force.

"Gerard Davison is going to buy a half-interest in the *Clarion,* and I am going to buy the other half. And I'm going to buy back his interest out of profits from the paper. I will be the editor and the publisher. Gerard will simply invest in a share of it. Does that strike you as a bad deal?"

"Of course not, and please don't yell at me!" Juliet told him frostily. "It's just that Gerard seems to be playing Santa Clause to all of Haleyville, and I was wondering if there was no limit to his operations. He gave the clinic a new ambulance, and we accepted it gratefully. So if he wants to give you a weekly newspaper, I see no reason he shouldn't. The *Clarion* isn't much of a paper. It was while Old Man Epperson lived. But when he died and his son took over, he didn't know how to run it, and it's just about gone to seed."

"You wait and see what I'm going to do with it," Steve boasted shamelessly, and added anxiously, "That is, of course, if I stay here."

"Well, aren't you?" asked Juliet, and would not meet his eyes.

"That's for you to decide," Steve told her quietly.

"Oh, but you must make that decision — " she protested.

Steve caught her by the shoulders and gave her an angry shake.

"Now don't you go coy on me, young woman!" he snapped. "You know perfectly well that I'm trying my darnedest to tell you that I love you and that I want to marry you and settle down in Haleyville. But if you won't marry me, then the heck with settling down in Haleyville."

Juliet pulled herself free of his hands and looked up at him, staying carefully out of his reach.

"This is undoubtedly the craziest proposal of marriage any girl ever had to listen to," she told him, and could not quite keep her voice steady for all her efforts.

"Well, I haven't had much experience in offering proposals of marriage," Steve defended himself. "This is the first one I ever made. You're probably an expert."

"Ha!" said Juliet scornfully. "I've read a few books!"

Steve made a little gesture of contemptuous dismissal.

"Oh, books!" he scoffed. "This is real, my girl. This is people — two people, you and me — and this is for life; not for a romantic novel. Now you tell me once and for all if you want to marry me. Do you?"

Juliet looked up into his eyes, and what she saw there made her heart gallop like a runaway horse. And evidently he saw something in her eyes that gave him encouragement, for he reached for her, and though she tried to step back a pace his arms caught her and held her close. He looked down into her uplifted face and asked in a voice that shook with a vibrant, aching tenderness, "Do you, Darling? Please say you do!"

Juliet drew a deep, ecstatic breath and gave him a radiant, dewy-eyed smile.

"Of course I do, dearest. More than anything else in the world, I want to marry you!" Her voice shook. And when he would have kissed her, she put up her hands and framed his face between them and held it away for just a moment. "But there's something you ought to know, Steve darling."

"All I need to know is that you love me."

"Oh, I do, dearest. I do. Wait — what I want to say is that you needn't come here to Haleyville. I'll go with you anywhere in the world you want to go, because anywhere with you would be my Shangri La!"

He looked down at her, deeply touched.

"Do you really mean that, sweet?" he asked.

"With all my heart," she said with beautiful simplicity.

"Why, thank you," said Steve in perfect seriousness, unable to find another phrase to express the joy he felt. "But the deal here in Haleyville with the *Clarion*, sweet, is the one thing I want, now that I know I have you! With you as my wife, and the *Clarion* as my job, I'll really have it made!"

And there was, of course, only one answer to that. And as Juliet lifted her mouth for his ardent kiss, she knew it was the answer he wanted.

Other titles in the Linford Romance Library:

A YOUNG MAN'S FANCY
Nancy Bell

Six people get together for reasons of their own, and the result is one of misunderstanding, suspicion and mounting tension.

THE WISDOM OF LOVE
Janey Blair

Barbie meets Louis and receives flattering proposals, but her reawakened affection for Jonah develops into an overwhelming passion.

MIRAGE IN THE MOONLIGHT
Mandy Brown

En route to an island to be secretary to a multi-millionaire, Heather's stubborn loyalty to her former flatmate plunges her into a grim hazard.

TENDER TYRANT
Quenna Tilbury

Candy's 'unofficial' fiancé met with an accident, and although she didn't love him, she felt she could not leave him now. But at the hospital she met the popular Brendan Birch!

TELEVISION SWEETHEART
Eileen Barry

The heart plays curious tricks, and it seems hard that Jill Harris could not reciprocate the love of Tiernan Wilde who adored her. Instead she finds herself yearning for Roger Thurlow whose past was shrouded in mystery.

DESERT DOCTOR
Violet Winspear

Madeline felt that Morocco was a place made for love and romance, but unfortunately Doctor Victor Tourelle seemed to be unaffected by its romantic spell.

ISLAND FIESTA
Jane Corrie

Corinne found herself trapped into marrying Juan Martel. He expected her to behave as a docile Spanish wife, and turn a blind eye to his affairs. How on earth could Corinne cope with this mess?

THE CORNISH HEARTH
Isobel Chace

Anna was not pleased when she ran into Piran Trethowyn again. She had no desire to further her acquaintance with such an insulting and overbearing character.

NOW WITH HIS LOVE
Hilda Nickson

Juliet hoped that Switzerland would help her to get over her broken engagement but all that happened was that she fell in love with Richard Thornton, who was not interested in her.

LAND OF TOMORROW
Mons Daveson

Nicola was going back to the little house on the coast near Brisbane. Would her future also contain Drew Huntley? He was certainly part of her present, whether she wanted him to be or not.

THE MAN AT KAMBALA
Kay Thorpe

Sara lived with her father at Kambala in Kenya and was accustomed to do as she pleased. She certainly didn't think much of Steve York who came to take charge in her father's absence.

ALLURE OF LOVE
Honor Vincent

Nerida Bayne took a winter sports holiday in Norway. After a case of mistaken identity, entanglements and heartache followed, but at last Nerida finds happiness.

THE MOUTH OF TRUTH
Isobel Chace

Deborah had hardly set foot in Rome before she was whisked away by Domenico Manzu, who kept her in his palace. But why?

PINK SNOW
Edna Dawe

In Austria, Kathryn Davies is soon caught up in a chain of events which lead to an attempt on her life. Soon it is apparent that the villagers of Mosskirch are conspiring to involve her in murder...

THE SIN OF CYNARA
Violet Winspear

Five-year-old Teri was not Carol's child but her sister Cynara's. She was determined to do her best for him, even if she had to beg the help of Vincenzo's family.

ACCIDENT CALL
Elizabeth Harrison

When the Accident Unit at St. Mark's heard they were getting a new house surgeon they were delighted. But Tim Harrington was something of a playboy. It took a serious motorway accident to make Tim "grow up".

BITTER HOMECOMING
Jan MacLean

Kathleen had always loved Adam Deerfield as a brother, but it was not long before she realised that her sisterly feeling had changed into a woman's love.

LOVE BE WARY
Mary Raymond

The holiday of a lifetime with no complications. But of course she hadn't bargained for Ben Eliot and Eddie Ricquier, nor for the stormy emotions the two men would arouse in her.

THE DIVIDED HOUSE
Mary Raymond

Sara Monroe was surprised to learn that she had only been left half of Great-Aunt Alicia's old house. The other half had been left to a young man who had been her aunt's tenant for just a few months . . .

ALMONER AT ANSON'S
Kathleen Treves

Brian Linguard, helpless after an accident, is worried about his daughter Annabel and Elizabeth Carradale offers to help. But defiant little Annabel soon shows where her heart lies . . .

TENDER TRUST
Kathleen Treves

Nurse Gay Holland had a 'way' with children — which was just as well when she found herself in charge of young Shirley Reve, after her father's accident.

THE VOICE OF MY LOVE
Pauline Ash

The car crash scarred and crippled her husband and small daughter. Was now the time to distress her husband further by cutting him out of her life.

RETURN TO LANMORE
Sheila Douglas

Nell's grandfather objected to her becoming a doctor. But now her grandfather was seriously ill and she had returned home to be with him.

REWARD OF LOVE
Quenna Tilbury

When Caroline's rich and eccentric employer died suddenly Caroline found she was to inherit a small legacy in return for doing some special jobs.